Lee Goes for Gold

Keith Charters

STRIDENT

www.stridentpublishing.co.uk

Published by
Strident Publishing Ltd
22 Strathwhillan Drive
East Kilbride
G75 8GT

Tel: +44 (0)1355 220588
info@stridentpublishing.co.uk
www.stridentpublishing.co.uk

JF

....

Print history
First published in 2006
This edition 2010

A catalogue record for this book is
available from the British Library.
ISBN 978-1-905537-25-9

Typeset in Gotham
Interior designed by Melvin Creative
Cover by Lawrence Mann
Printed by JF Print

Keith Charters

has lived all over the UK, and now lives near Glasgow. He studied at the University of Strathclyde and should have gained a first class honours degree, but missed out by half a percent, mainly because he was playing snooker when he should have been studying. (Let this be a lesson to all.)

After graduating, Keith worked in various business management roles, ending up in London, where he headed up part of a big, rather strange, financial company in which staff got paid for shouting at their customers ... and at each other. It was weird.

At this point Keith started writing a lot. An awful lot. Soon writing was taking over his life. So he took a deep breath, gave up his 'proper' job and began writing full-time.

Lee and the Consul Mutants was the first fruit of his labours. It took the no.1 spot in *The Herald's* Children's Bestsellers chart during 2006, with *Lee Goes For Gold* no.4 at the same time. Keith never looked back. Out came *Lee's Holiday Showdown* followed by *Lee on the Dark Side of the Moon*. However, you can read the Lee novels in any order you like.

As well as writing, Keith now visits over 100 schools, libraries and book festivals each year and is renowned for his hilarious and energetic events. If you would like to invite Keith to visit your school, email him at:

keith@keithcharters.co.uk

For Mum and Dad

Chapter
One

Lee found the invitation to *Bring-Your-Kids-to-Work Day* on the kitchen table and charged upstairs to find his dad.

'Dad, do they have *Bring-Your-Kids-to-Work Day* every year?' he shouted through the bathroom door.

'This is the first one,' his dad called back. 'Why?'

'I can't wait to see what your work is like.'

It was an enthusiasm that his dad didn't seem to share. 'You don't *really* want to go, do you? It's only an office,' he told Lee. 'An office is an office is an office. It's really not very exciting.'

'It will be, Dad! Can I go? Can I?'

Lee's dad's voice was muffled. 'I'm about to get into the shower.'

'I know, Dad, but can I go?'

'I don't know ....'

Lee recognised a sign of weakness when he heard one and leapt to make the most of his opportunity.

'Honestly, Dad, it'll be brilliant! I've never been to where you work. And it'll be a great chance for us to spend some quality time together like Mum's always saying we should.'

'But like I've said, Lee, it's only an office. You'll be bored silly ...'

'No I won't, Dad. I promise.'

Lee continued cajoling his dad for several minutes longer. Finally his dad gave in and agreed, mainly so he could enjoy some peace and quiet relaxing in the shower after a hard day at work.

If only he'd known then the effect his decision would have.

Lee felt a pang of excitement as he stepped off the early morning train. He and his dad made their way down the platform, along with hundreds of other workers, before exiting the station and crossing a busy city centre street.

Visiting his dad's office made him feel important, and he held his head high with pride.

Of course, Lee's main reason for wanting to visit wasn't to see where his dad worked or to spend quality time with him; it was to get out of school for a day. Any excuse to escape his teacher, Mrs Ogilvy (better known as The Ogre), was, in Lee's opinion, a good excuse. And as excuses went, this was a cracker. No Maths, no Language and no Re - ligious Education; instead, a day spent lounging about a plush office, watching people work and hopefully getting a chance to play on the powerful computers his dad was always talking about.

However, he was genuinely interested to find out what his dad did all day. He knew he was an Internal Audit Manager, but wasn't sure what that job title entailed. He'd asked before, but his dad had never explained it very well. Did he go to lots of important meetings? Did he make lots of crucial decisions and phone calls? And, most important of all, did he hire and fire people and boss them about a lot? Lee hoped so.

As they fought their way along the crowded pavements Lee watched the bustle around them.

'Well here it is. This is where I spend most of my life when I'm not at home with you and Mum and Rebecca,' Lee's dad announced as they arrived outside a tall, imposing building, one way bigger than Lee's school and much more impressive.

'Morning,' said a man in a black uniform as Lee and his dad entered through a gleaming revolving door.

'Morning, Dennis,' Lee's dad responded.

'Who's he?' Lee asked as they strode on. 'A policeman?'

'No, no. Well, yes, I suppose so. In a way. Kind of.'

'Eh?' Lee said.

'He's Dennis – the security guard.'

'Oh.'

'He makes sure that only those who're supposed to get in actually do.'

'How does he know who's supposed to get in?'

'He knows people's faces.'

'But there are hundreds of people in your office.'

Lee's dad grinned. 'He's got a good memory.'

He'd need to have, Lee thought. Dennis The Amazing Memory Man. He ought to be on stage, not hanging around office doorways.

Loads of other people were making their way into the building. Some had their heads down as if trying to avoid speaking to anyone, others were chatting away as if work was the last thing on their mind – which it probably was.

Lee and his dad joined the queue outside the lifts. Lee was wary of lifts. Last time he'd been in one it had taken him through a portal for an encounter with some mutants. But that was another story. This time his main concern was breathing, and seeing what was going on. Everyone was taller than him; his head just reached the shoulders of the smaller women. It was as well he wasn't scared of confined spaces. What was that called? Claustrophobia, that was it. He remembered because he used to think it meant a fear of Santa Claus.

There was a ding from the lift as they reached the first floor.

'How many floors are there?' Lee whispered to his dad.

'Twelve.'

'Will it stop at every one?'

'Probably. It usually does at this time of day.'

Lee hoped none of the passengers in the lift had eaten curry the previous night. In such a tight huddle no-one would survive a serious bottom burp.

More and more people exited the lift as they rose higher and higher up the building. By the time they reached the eleventh floor there were just five people left.

'Morning, Sanjeev,' Lee's dad said to one of the others, a man with so little hair on his head that he surely got half price at the barber's.

'Hi, Pete,' the man replied. 'This your youngster, then?'

'Yes, this is Lee.'

'Ah,' Sanjeev said, then looked down at Lee. 'Come to check up on your dad, have you?'

'Why, what's he done wrong?'

'Nothing that I'm aware of,' Sanjeev said.

'Sanjeev's just being funny,' Lee's dad explained.

'Oh, right. I thought maybe you were in trouble for

bringing home that box of paper and all those pens and pencils ...'

Lee was cut off in mid-sentence by a loud cough from his dad, immediately followed by another ding from the lift.

Sanjeev laughed as they stepped out of the lift. 'I see he's got your sense of humour,' he remarked to Lee's dad.

This news alarmed Lee. His dad had a dreadful sense of humour. He was always telling terrible jokes and finding things funny that no sane person could possibly consider amusing.

'I hope not,' Lee said.

That only made Sanjeev laugh even more before he headed off in the opposite direction.

'Don't mention that I take stuff home,' Lee's dad said as soon as Sanjeev was out of earshot. 'I'm not supposed to.'

'You mean you steal it?'

'I wouldn't call it stealing ... Oh, now here's the photocopier,' Lee's dad said, trying to change the subject faster than a team of mechanics replacing the tyres on a Formula 1 car.

'Well, it's not borrowing, Dad, because you never take any of it back ...'

Lee's dad lost his usual calm. 'It's a perk of the job, okay,

Lee! Nobody misses the odd pen or piece of paper.'

'Okay, Dad,' Lee decided to agree, realising he was winding him up.

'Good.' His Dad took a deep breath to calm himself. 'Now I'll show you around so you can get your bearings.'

On the outside of Lee's dad's office door was a sign that said:

> ## PETER WATERS
> ### INTERNAL AUDIT MANAGER

Whatever it meant, that was what Lee's dad was.

The office was small. Small but bright, because it was an office with a window, which Lee decided meant his dad was important.

'What can I do?' Lee asked as they entered.

'Listen and learn,' his dad replied.

His dad then spent half an hour on the telephone running through a load of numbers with whoever was on the other end of the line.

Fascinating stuff. NOT! As far as Lee could make out, work was duller than school.

And if by 'listen and learn' his dad meant he should remember all those numbers, then he had to be joking.

Not even Dennis The Amazing Memory Man could remember all those. And what use would they be anyway?

About halfway through the morning Lee's dad declared, 'Right, let's go.'

'Go where?'

'To meet the other kids.'

Lee had been wondering where they were all hiding. He'd only seen two since arriving and was desperate to find out if everyone else was finding it all as dreary as he was.

Lee followed his dad along a corridor. Several people said 'hi' as they passed.

'It's the people that make work interesting,' Lee's dad told him as they walked the entire length of the building, 'not just the work itself. It would be boring going through the motions without others to speak to.'

'So why do you have an office to yourself then? Why don't you sit with the others?'

'Because I'm a manager.'

'But I thought that was a good thing?'

'It is.'

'Then why do they split you up from everyone else and make it boring for you?'

'Sometimes I need the privacy.'

'Aw,' Lee said, though he was none the wiser.

They eventually arrived outside big double doors, on which a sign said,

BOARD ROOM

Given his experience of work so far, Lee wondered if the signwriter had made a spelling mistake. *Bored Room* seemed more appropriate.

Inside were twenty adults and a similar number of children. The adults were all talking to each other and looking proud of their sons and daughters. However, it was clear to Lee that most of those sons and daughters were more interested in the free drinks and cakes on offer than in meeting their parent's colleagues. And Lee didn't blame them. Free food and drink was always worthy of interest.

But before he could make a start on the tempting feast, a well-dressed man in a dark blue suit entered the room, drawing the attention of most of the adults. He possessed the most amazing eyebrows; great big bushy clumps of fluffy hair, as if someone had stuck two dead hamsters just below his forehead. If he ever went bald he could brush them backwards to cover the whole of his head. (Okay, so he'd have a very unusual fringe ....)

Lee and his dad were closest to the new arrival.

'Hi, Peter,' he said to Lee's dad. 'And who's this?'

'This is my son, Lee.'

'Pleased to meet you, Lee,' the man said, holding out a hand. 'I'm Wayne Scales.'

Lee took the hand that was offered and shook it, doing his best not to snigger at the man's name.

'Mr Scales owns and runs the company,' Lee's dad told Lee, raising his eyebrows in a so-be-on-your-best-behaviour-my-job-might-depend-on-it way.

'So what do you want to do when you grow up?' Mr Scales asked. 'Have you got what it takes to become a successful businessman?'

'I don't really know,' Lee said. 'How do you become one?'

'By working hard at school,' Lee's dad was quick to point out.

'That, certainly,' Mr Scales said. 'But it's partly an attitude. You need to have some imagination so you can come up with ideas to make money, and then you've got to have the confidence to see them through. If you've got those, and a bit of common sense, then there's nothing to stop you.'

'How did you start off?' Lee asked, warming to Mr Scales.

'I was just going to tell that story to everyone here, so why don't you grab a cake and get a coffee for your dad, and then I'll crack on.'

Knowing how quickly cake can go off when left out of an airtight container, Lee did the decent thing and helped himself to a slice ... and then to another one. He also took a drink to flush it down, as well as the suggested coffee for his dad. He quickly swallowed the first slice of cake so that he wouldn't get told off for being greedy.

By then, Mr Scales had shaken more hands than the Queen on a walkabout. He stepped up onto a small, raised platform and everyone turned to face him.

'Well, good morning everyone,' he began. There was a rumble of response like Lee's classmates saying good morning to The Ogre. Except that no-one was calling Mr Scales names under their breath.

'Welcome to Scales Insurance. For those of you I haven't already met, I'm Wayne Scales, founder of the company.' Mr Scales seemed completely at ease speaking to so many people at once. He was clearly used to it.

'Now, I was going to tell you all about the way we run our worldwide operations, but I decided that might be rather dull. After all, the whole point of today is to inspire young people like you to want to go into business, so that hopefully one day you'll create companies like ours.

'So, what I propose to do instead is tell you a little about how this company came into being.'

At first Lee wasn't sure if this would be any more riveting than hearing about its worldwide operations, but the more he listened the more interested he became.

Wayne Scales explained that he'd had a perfectly normal childhood. He'd worked hard at school, but had also spent plenty of time playing with other kids, and there was nothing wrong with that, he said. The most important skill a person could develop was how to get on with others, because in business a lot of time was spent working in teams.

Mr Scales hadn't known what he wanted to do when he left school. When he was younger he'd fancied being a fireman or an astronaut or a footballer. But by the time he was seventeen those notions had passed. After sitting all his exams he took a summer job as a postman while waiting to find out if a college or university would accept him. One finally did, but by then he'd become used to earning a wage, so decided to carry on working.

He managed to get a full-time job at an insurance

company. 'To begin with,' he said, 'because I'd been a postman, I was given a job in the mail room—a room where women aren't allowed ...' There were a few polite chuckles at Mr Scales's joke before he explained that the mail room was of course where the post went before being distributed throughout the company.

Mr Scales quickly noticed lots of things he thought could be improved in the mail room, so one night he wrote them all down, along with his proposed solutions. The next day he asked to see a director and showed him his ideas. The director liked them so much that he gave him an office and made it his job to put the ideas into practice.

The young Mr Scales found he had a flair for coming up with ideas, and started to develop more, including some for how the company could sell additional insurance policies to existing customers. Not all of the ideas were successful, but most of them made a difference, and over the course of ten years Mr Scales was promoted up through the company until he became its youngest ever chief executive, complete with a fancy car.

'Then, after two years in that job,' he said, 'I decided to leave.'

Lee looked up at his dad and noticed that several other kids were also looking quizzically at their parents. *Why?*

they all wanted to know. Why had Mr Scales decided to quit when he'd just become top dog, king of the hill, master of the universe?

'The reason I left,' Mr Scales explained, as if reading their minds, 'was that I wanted to prove I could do it all for myself. There's a big difference between being the boss of a company that already exists and setting one up yourself. A big big difference. But I managed it. And the result is what you'll have seen walking around this office today: a company that employs seven-hundred-and-eighty staff in this building alone, and that has grown to become one of the most successful insurance companies in the world.'

Lee was impressed. This guy was good. He knew what he wanted and knew how to go about getting it.

'So that's my story, short and simple. And what I'd like you to remember from it is this: use whatever skills you have. If you're good at making things, then make things. If you're good at painting, then paint things. And if you have a good imagination, use it to come up with ideas for improving what you see around you.'

Mr Scales nodded his thanks for the ripple of applause that greeted the end of his speech. He then stepped back into the midst of the throng. A moment later, before Lee had even had time to grab a third slice of cake, Mr Scales was back in front of him.

'So, was that interesting?' Mr Scales asked.

Lee nodded.

'Good. And what do you think was the key message? What did you take from my story?'

Lee thought about this. Was it that a) all aspiring astronauts should become postmen? b) you get a fancy car if you become the boss? c) you shouldn't waste your talents? or d) eating two slices of cake very quickly makes you feel ill?

Lee wasn't very good at multiple-choice questions.

'C,' Lee said, guessing.

'What?' asked his dad.

Lee realised his mistake. 'Eh, see that you don't waste your talents.'

'Excellent, excellent.' Mr Scales seemed really pleased. 'That's exactly what I wanted to get across.'

A hand landed on Lee's shoulder. It was his dad's, and it meant he was proud of Lee.

'You'll go far if you recognise that,' Mr Scales said.

'Thanks,' Lee told him. 'I've heard that Australia's well worth a visit ....'

Lee's mum was upstairs trying to persuade his four-year-old sister Rebecca to get ready for bed, while Lee was sitting in the kitchen with his dad, eating supper after their long day at the office.

'Is Mr Scales incredibly rich?' Lee asked.

'Fairly.'

'Richer than the Queen?'

'Not richer than the Queen, no. But then Mr Scales has worked hard to earn what he's made, not inherited a load of palaces and paintings that ought to belong to the nation. You see, the problem with the monarchy is ...'

'Eh, Dad ... I was only asking if he's richer than her.'

Lee's dad blushed. 'Oh right, sorry about that. I was almost off on a rant there, wasn't I?'

'Yes, but that's okay, because you sort of answered my question.'

Lee's dad was always banging on about the Queen and politics. He would often shout at people on the radio or television, even though they couldn't hear him. But, Lee didn't mind. Listening to others was a good way of learning about the world, and Lee thought some of his dad's ideas were actually quite good.

'Have you been to Mr Scales's house?' Lee asked.

'No.'

'I'll bet it's huge.'

'I imagine it's fabulous.'

Lee could imagine that, too. Indeed he'd spent a good part of the afternoon doing so. Mr Scales's house would have loads of rooms and an Olympic-size swimming pool and a gym and TVs everywhere and a butler to open the door for you and get you whatever you wanted whenever you wanted it; and the garden would be so big that you'd need a quad bike to get around it, which would be sooooo cool.

And all because Mr Scales had a good imagination. Well, Lee had a good imagination too. People were always telling him so. 'Lee,' they'd say (because that was his name), 'Lee, that really is some imagination you've got.' And yet they always made it sound as if it was a bad thing. Well more fool them. It had served Mr Scales well, now it was Lee's turn.

Lee felt inspired. *He* could be the next Mr Scales! Why not? All he needed to do was to use his imagination to come up with a brilliant business idea.

So he put his thinking cap on.

Lee was still wearing his thinking cap a week later. He'd been thinking very hard for every one of the seven days and so far had failed to come up with a single brilliant idea. He was beginning to think he wasn't cut out to be a high-powered businessman after all. Maybe he'd need to settle for being a window cleaner (except he was scared of heights) or a teacher (except he didn't relish teaching children with an attention span like his own) or a zoo keeper (except he didn't fancy cleaning out elephants' toilets).

Then finally the idea came.

It came shortly after his mum arrived home. When she saw the state of his bedroom (which admittedly was bad, even by Lee's standards) she told him in no uncertain terms to 'get it sorted.' Most of the mess was old toys he'd strewn across the floor while emptying his cupboards to find the newer toys he actually wanted to play with. However, his mum's nagging to tidy up set him thinking. What was he keeping those old toys for? He didn't play with most of them; they just clogged up his cupboards and made it difficult to find things. What if he was to sell them?

But never mind *What if?* because *How much?* was the

more important question. How much could he get rid of, and how much money could he make as a result?

He spent all evening in his room rummaging through his cupboards and placing similar toys together in piles around the floor; Lego in one pile, Action Man gear in another and so on. He even neatly stacked his old comics, of which there were many more than he'd realised.

When he was nearly finished he began to think about the best way of selling his worldly possessions. Should he advertise them in the local newspaper? Should he hang posters at school or on lampposts near his house? Or …

'Dad, can we have a yard sale?'

'I'm not sure we've got much to sell.'

'I have.'

'Have you?'

Lee explained what he'd spent the last few hours doing.

'Well, Mum will be pleased to see some of that clutter go. But why don't you just give it all to a jumble sale?'

'Because then someone else will make all the money from it, not me.'

'That's not so bad, is it? It'd be for a good cause.'

'Dad, *I'm* a good cause. And this is business, not charity. I bought some of those toys with my birthday and pocket money.'

'Let me speak to Mum about it.'

'Does that mean I can have one?'

'It means I want to speak to Mum about it. But good try. You should be one of those political interviewers on the radio. You've certainly got the dogged persistence for it.'

Lee's mum was out at a friend's house and wouldn't be back until Lee was asleep. He would have to wait until the morning for his parents' final decision.

Of course, even if his mum and dad did agree to him holding a yard sale, selling his old toys could only be a start. It might raise a little money, but once the toys were gone, that would be it. What he really needed was a regular income – money every week or every fortnight. And the next day, which was a Saturday, he spotted a perfect opportunity.

It's incredible how quickly a brilliant mind can work. All those electrical pulses in the brain linking up to create more thoughts in a second than the brainiest computer can process in a lifetime. And, back when brains were being given out, Lee was up there at the front of the queue.

As Lee stepped out of the front door, intending to head to the house of his best friend, Will, he saw his eccentric next-door neighbour, Holly Arthanthou, preparing to clean her car as she did religiously every Saturday morning.

Holly lived alone, and once you knew her it wasn't difficult to understand why. She was an old fusspot with a strong dislike of mess, noise and any sort of change to her routines. When every house in the area was sent a letter explaining that the weekly bin collection was being moved from Tuesday to Wednesday, it was as if the end of the world had been announced. Or so Lee's dad had said one evening at dinner after he'd bumped into Holly and she'd subjected him to her woe on the subject. Lee generally kept his distance from her. He was polite, but avoided lengthy conversations because they could be very lengthy once Holly got started. But this morning he was more than happy to speak to her.

'Morning, Holly,' Lee said as he walked down the drive from his house. 'It's a lovely day.'

'It is, too,' she replied. 'And here's me having to spend it washing this car when I ought to be out enjoying my back garden, which of course is where all the sun is. But it has to be done. I can't be seen out and about in a dirty car.'

Personally, Lee didn't see why not – it was what his family had been doing for as long as he could remember – but he was alive to the opportunity. 'Maybe I could help you,' he offered. 'Maybe I could wash your car each week so that you could spend more time in your back garden, enjoying the sun and the pleasant smell from your wonderful display of colourful flowers.'

'Oh no, I couldn't have you doing that! I'd be holding you back from playing with your friends.'

Lee decided not to explain that he had precisely one

friend, namely Will. It would make him sound almost as sad as her. No-one ever came to her house, not unless you counted the postman, but it would be pushing it a bit to call him a 'friend'.

'I wouldn't mind, not if it meant I could earn a little extra pocket-money,' Lee said, hoping he wasn't sounding too blunt.

'Would you really be interested?' Holly queried. 'I wouldn't mind paying you. After all, it would cost me a few pounds if I were to take it to the car wash.'

'You're right. Those car washes are a rip-off. I'm sure I could do a much better job than them.'

'Well, I suppose ...'

Thirty seconds later the deal was done.

Lee hadn't told Will he was coming round, so he dropped that idea and instead washed Holly's car before she could change her mind.

Holly kept fussing ('Do you want some more washing liquid? Make sure that water isn't so hot that it burns you!'). Eventually Lee said, in the friendliest tone he could manage, 'Holly, why don't you go into your garden and leave me to it, because otherwise you won't benefit from me doing this.'

'Oh well, yes, I suppose you're right. I should really,

shouldn't I?' With that she picked up a fold-away seat and carried it round to her patio.

Holly's car was small, so it didn't take Lee very long to clean it. As it was the first time he'd washed it, he decided to wipe it with a shammy cloth so it wouldn't end up all smudgy when it dried properly. Given how fussy Holly was, Lee considered this worthwhile. If ever there was a time to do a great job it was the first time, because that way you could ensure there would be second and third and fourth times.

Eventually, once he was satisfied that the car was shining sufficiently brightly, Lee carried the bucket and sponge round to the back of the house. 'That's it done,' he announced to Holly.

'Oh that's great. Thanks ever so much, Lee.' She scuttled off into the kitchen and returned a few seconds later with Lee's first ever wage. 'Here you go. I hope this is enough.'

It was more than enough, but obviously Lee didn't say that.

'So is it okay if I wash your car *every* Saturday?' Lee checked, just to make sure she'd understood the deal they'd struck. 'I could do it even if you're still in bed. I'll just use the water from our kitchen.

'Oh that would be marvellous! I'm really getting too old

24

to be undertaking these sorts of strenuous activities myself. At my age I should be relaxing and making the most of the time I have left.'

Holly was always going on like this, as if she were a hundred and ten years old, frail and liable to keel over at any moment. The truth was that she had only just turned fifty and was as fit as a fiddle because she couldn't stop fidgeting. She was forever tidying up, cleaning or just moving things around for the sake of it. But Lee wasn't about to convince his first paying customer that she was doing the wrong thing, no matter how nutty it seemed to him.

On Monday morning, on the way to school, Lee saw Mr Upa Blin Dali out working in his garden.

Lee knew Mr Dali spent very long hours running his small restaurant, and it was immediately clear to Lee that the poor man shouldn't also have to be working all the rest of the hours of the day slogging away in his garden. No, he ought to be paying someone else to do that instead. Say ... Lee, for instance. It would benefit both of them—Mr Dali could save his energy for work, thus keeping his customers happy and earning more money than he'd need to pay Lee to keep his garden tidy for him; and Lee would be making more money too. It was a simple matter of economics.

Lee decided to seize upon this early-morning opportunity. He leaned over the gate and called, 'Morning, Mr Dali.'

Mr Dali looked up.

'Morning, Lee. Is that you off to school?'

'Yes. I see you're working hard on your garden.'

'Yes, I am. It is a pain in the ... well, you can guess where, I am sure. But it has to be done, otherwise the place looks a mess and I don't want that. Got to be respectable, you know.'

'Yes, but you work so hard in your restaurant, Mr Dali. You should get someone else to do that for you.'

'Ah, you are so right, young Lee. I should. But the problem is, where would I find a reliable person at a reasonable rate of pay?'

'Well now, Mr Dali, you know it's funny you should mention that ...'

'Now then, if you'll turn to page thirty-seven of *Maths Is Fun* ...' The Ogre barked.

Yasmin, the girl sitting next to Lee, nudged him.

'Eh?'

'Page thirty-seven of your Maths book,' she whispered.

'Oh, right. Thanks.'

Lee had been away on another planet. It hadn't even been a nearby one, rather a tiny speck on the edge of the solar system, somewhere beyond Pluto. His burgeoning business empire had been occupying his thoughts. Gardening, washing cars ... well, okay, that was all it was so far, but there would be more in due course. It might be an idea to hire a secretary, and he was just thinking about asking Yasmin, who was always alert and efficient, when The Ogre pounced on him.

'So, Lee. Number two?'

'No need, Miss. I went before school.'

The class burst into laughter.

'That's enough!' The Ogre shouted as she approached Lee's desk. She leaned over and breathed into his face.

Whatever she'd had for breakfast that day had been a LONG way past its Use By date. 'Lee, I have no interest whatsoever in your toilet habits. *Question* number two. What is the answer to it?'

'Oh, question two ...'

He was tapped on his foot under the table. Then again and again and once more. 'Four,' Lee told The Ogre when he was sure the tapping had stopped.

She was shocked that he'd come up with the right answer. 'Eh, that's right,' she said, almost as if she were disappointed not to have caught him out. She moved on and picked on someone else.

'Thanks,' Lee mouthed to Yasmin, whose tapping had saved him from any embarrassment. He would try to help her out sometime to repay the favour.

Lee returned to working out how many gardens he could dig, and how many cars he could wash, in a normal week. Then he calculated how much money he could make from those two activities. The answer was: quite a lot.

But still, he was going to have to work hard for it all, and he wasn't too keen on that. There had to be an easier way, a way in which other people would do the hard work for him but he would make money from their efforts. After all, that was what Mr Scales did. He couldn't do everything in the company on his own – there weren't enough hours in the day – so he hired others to do the real work; all he actually did was mastermind everything. He came up with ideas and organised everyone else to put them into practice.

Could Lee do the same? Could he organise a squad of kids to wash cars and dig gardens but take a share of their earnings?

It was certainly an idea worth thinking about.

So Lee thought about it.

The neighbours were proving to be a ready source of income for Lee. First there was washing Holly Arthanthou's car, and now he had agreed to tidy Upa Blin Dali's garden every second week for a couple of hours, starting just as soon as Lee and Rebecca returned from Uncle Raymond's the following weekend.

There were opportunities on his doorstep, Lee realised, it was just a case of keeping his eyes open to make sure he spotted them.

He stood at the front window and eyed up each nearby house in turn, thinking about the way the inhabitants lived and about their particular pet hates and loves.

Aha! That was it! Pet hates. Pet loves. Pets!

Al Satian, the man two houses down the hill, had a large and, to Lee's mind, very stupid dog called Rogan (named after Al's favourite curry – rogan josh), a red setter that wasn't really red, more copper-brown. Al loved his dog to bits, but he had a small garden, a young family, a demanding job and a partner who also worked, so he found it difficult to make time to take Rogan for walks.

Could Lee persuade Al to pay him to walk Rogan?

Perhaps not every day, but maybe on the days when Al or his partner weren't able to walk the dog themselves – which seemed to be most days.

On the face of it this seemed like a great idea, but Lee did have a couple of reservations. The first was that Rogan whined a lot. An awful lot. Whine, whine, whine. It was like listening to The Ogre, except that she went whinge, whinge, whinge (which, interestingly, was just 'whine' with an added 'g'). Rogan was also inclined to sit on people's feet, supposedly as a sign of affection.

But worse than either Rogan's whining or his sitting on feet was his slobbering. When he got going he was a real slobbering champion. Long, stringy, gooey, gungy, sticky, manky slavers of white stuff would hang down from the sides of his mouth. There was no need for that, Lee reckoned. It was one thing for Rogan to feel hungry; it was quite another for him to put the rest of the world off its dinner. Worst of all, though, was when Rogan shook his head, sending the gobby goo all over the place, and all over anyone who happened to be standing within range. (And range in Rogan's case was about ten metres.)

However, in the interests of making money anything could be overlooked or overcome. Lee could always wear waterproofs if the slobbering became unbearable, just so long as he earned an income.

He would speak to Al later that evening, after dinner.

It was raining during morning interval at school, which meant pupils weren't allowed out, though at least they were allowed into neighbouring classrooms to see their friends. So Lee sat next to Will, who had a carton of milk in front of him.

'I'm starving,' Lee said.

'Me too,' Will agreed. 'And it's still ages until lunchtime.'

'The school should have a tuck shop where you can go if you're about to die of hunger. Somewhere to get emergency rations to keep you alive.'

Lee sucked the milk up his straw, then blew it back down again to make it last longer and generate bubbles.

Then he stopped. He stopped sucking at the straw and he stopped blowing down it.

He'd had an idea.

'Why *don't* we have a tuck shop?' Lee enthused.

'Eh ... I don't know.'

'Why *can't* we have one?'

Will thought about this for a second, but said, 'Eh ... I don't know that one either.'

'There's no reason, is there? No reason at all! But that doesn't mean we shouldn't have one. Or that we can't have one.'

'So what are you going to do? Are you going to ask The Ogre if you can open one?'

'No ...'

'The headmistress, then?'

'No ...'

'The janitor?'

'No ...'

'Lee, you're doing that 'no' thing again and it's very annoying ...'

'Sorry.'

'So who are you going to ask?'

'No-one.'

'Yeah, but you'd still need to ask ...'

Lee stopped him. 'Not if it's *my* tuck shop.'

'But how can it be if it's in the school?'

'Easy! I'll buy the stuff, and I'll bring it in each day, then people can buy direct from me.'

Lee was excited. He'd used his imagination, just as Mr Scales had, and had come up with a brilliant idea. He was so impressed that he would have given himself a slap on the back had his arm been long enough to reach.

'This week a school tuck shop, next week ...' He wondered where it might all lead ... A proper shop in town ... then a chain of shops that he would float on the stock exchange. Expansion into America with mainland Europe to follow ... then a knighthood, so everyone would have to call him Sir Lee. He didn't even care that his dad wouldn't like him receiving his knighthood from the Queen.

'Are you going to do it all by yourself?' Will asked.

'Do you want to help?'

'Okay.'

'Wow! I'm already employing staff!'

'What will my job be?' Will asked.

'Well, I'll need to be chief executive, so you can be ... shop assistant.'

'Oh.'

'Or,' Lee said, recognising Will's disappointment, 'maybe you should be manager.'

A smile crawled across Will's face. 'Manager,' he repeated, trying out the title on himself. 'Cool!'

'But I'll need to get the business going first before I actually need to employ any staff.'

'That's okay. I can wait.'

'It's a deal then.'

And they shook hands on it, just like real businessmen.

But even as their sweaty palms joined, all was not well. Out of the corner of his roving eye Lee caught sight of a face peering down at them. An adult face, he was sure, but it was gone before his brain could process the features and work out who it was. Was one of the teachers onto him? Surely not. How could he have given himself away already? He hadn't even started! He'd only just had the idea a couple of minutes beforehand and hadn't even finished shaking hands with Will. And shaking hands could mean anything. They could be making up after a disagreement, or playing at being businessmen, or agreeing to swap computer games; entirely innocent activities that teachers didn't need to go poking their noses into and didn't need to peek out of windows to check up on.

However, Lee suspected some teachers were mind-readers. They certainly had an uncanny ability to tell you not to do something even before you'd thought of doing it in the first place. And Lee knew that if the teachers did find out what he was up to they would try to stop him.

He needed to be on his guard.

That evening Lee knocked on Al Satian's front door. As he stood waiting for it to be answered, he was able to inspect the great many paw marks that had removed most of the paint from it. At the same time he was able to consider what damage those same claws might do to a human being; say, for instance, an eleven-year-old boy who wanted to walk the dog that owned those claws.

Al's partner, Joanne, answered. 'Hi Lee. How are you?'

Before Lee was able to reply he was knocked into a rosemary bush by a dog torpedo. Rogan had arrived and carried straight on, regardless of Lee's presence.

'Oh dear, sorry. Are you okay?' Joanne helped Lee out of the bush, the leaves of which had left him smelling like a lamb chop fresh out of the oven.

'Eh, yeah. I think so.'

'Rogan!' Joanne shouted. 'Come here.' Rogan's head dropped and he slowly walked back to the door. 'Now, apologise to Lee. That was very bad.'

'Sorry,' Rogan said.

Well, no, obviously he didn't actually say that. But his big, sad eyes did make it look as if he was sorry.

'Actually,' said Lee, 'I came round to ask if you'd like me to take Rogan for walks when you can't manage it. I know it's not easy to fit them in when you both work and have your children to look after, and I'm too young to do a paper round, so I thought maybe if you could pay me a little for walking him instead ....'

'Oh, well, now that's an idea. Are you sure you really want to, especially after ... you know, what he did to you a moment ago.'

Lee's brain wanted to say, 'No', but his mouth wanted to say, 'Yes'. 'Nes', was what came out.

'Nes?'

'I mean yes. Yes, I'll happily walk Rogan as often as you want.'

Rogan's head lifted sharply, as if he could work out what was being said but thought he'd better keep quiet so people didn't realise he could understand them.

'Well that would be great. I'm sure Rogan would love it. But are you sure your parents won't mind?'

'I'll check with them, but I'm sure it'll be okay. They'll be happy for me to get the exercise.'

'Just as we'll be happy to see Rogan get some, too,' Joanne said, risking slobbers by rubbing the dog's chin. 'It's a deal.'

Chapter
Five

' Mum,' Lee said later that afternoon while eating a biscuit. 'Where do shopkeepers buy their sweets from?'

'Spray that again.'

'What?'

'You've just sprayed biscuit everywhere. You should wait until you've swallowed your food before speaking.'

Lee quickly swallowed the masticated mush in his mouth. 'But do you know, Mum?'

'From a cash and carry, I suppose. Why?'

Experience had taught Lee that asking further questions nearly always distracted adults from pursuing answers to their own queries. It was a technique he tried now because he wasn't ready to explain his idea to his mum, not just yet.

'What's a cash and carry?' he asked.

'It's a sort of warehouse where shopkeepers buy in bulk. Why, what's all this about?'

'What does "buying in bulk" mean, Mum? Does it mean only fat shopkeepers can buy there?'

'It means buying lots of something to get it cheaper. Instead of buying a few packets of crisps, you can buy a whole box of them there and that way it costs less per packet. That's how shopkeepers make a profit; they buy more cheaply than they sell for.'

'How much profit do they make?'

Lee's mum chuckled. 'I've no idea, Poppet! That all depends.'

Lee munched on another biscuit. Soon his mum would remind him not to eat the tin as well, like she always did. And not without good reason.

He had to get into a cash and carry, he decided. It didn't take a genius to work out that if he bought sweets from a small local shop he would only be able to sell them for about the same as he paid for them. If he tried to sell them for more, customers would just go to that local shop instead, because they'd know it was cheaper.

'Can anyone go to a cash and carry?' Lee asked.

'I think you have to be a member first.'

'Aw.'

This was very bad news. How was he going to get into one if he had to be a member first? Break in? Sneak in on the back of a lorry?

Going through the door would certainly be much easier, but he had no idea how he could arrange that. Not unless he came clean and told his mum and dad of his brilliant plan to run a mobile tuck shop.

Lee's mum and dad were always trying to get the whole family – themselves, Lee and Rebecca – to sit down together for dinner. It was important that they communicated regularly, so they said. That way they could maintain harmony in their family unit. Lee thought that sounded like psychobabble and usually itched to jump down from his seat so he could return to his favourite cartoons. But not today. Today he had an important and potentially life-changing announcement to make.

'Mum ... Dad ... I've got an important and potentially life-changing announcement to make,' he began (predictably).

'What about me?' Rebecca asked.

'Eh, yeah, I suppose you, too.'

'Go on, tell us what it is. Is it a "Very Good" in your Maths?'

Unlikely. Not without some clever photocopying or scanning of other pupils' answers.

'No, no, nothing like that.'

'What then? Have you been chosen to play the lead in the school play?'

That was equally improbable.

'No.'

'Lee ...'

'I'm going to start a business.'

'Oh ... right.' Lee's dad stopped chewing his food, and his mum held her fork still, halfway to her open mouth.

'It was Mr Scales who inspired me,' Lee explained, thinking this would win favour with his dad. In fact it was his mum who was delighted.

'Oh, that's great,' she said. She turned to her husband. 'You see, I told you it would be worthwhile taking Lee to *Bring-Your-Kids-to-Work Day*. You should take him next year as well.'

Lee's dad didn't look altogether convinced.

'Yes, I'm going to set up a tuck shop at school,' Lee said, 'because everyone's always starving and there's nowhere to get any food, so it should be really popular.'

'Ah,' his dad said in a way that didn't sound promising. 'Eh, Lee, much as I admire your entrepreneurial spirit and want to encourage it ...' At that point he looked over the table at Lee's mum, silently communicating with her as if they were telepathic, which Lee was convinced they actually were. '... I mean, it's good that you're interested in business and whatnot – that's the reason I volunteered to take you into the office, after all ...'

There was something about his dad's tone that suggested to Lee that his big announcement was about to become a big flop. He just knew that his dad was about to say 'but'.

'... but,' his dad went on, 'I think at this point in your school life it's more important that you concentrate on your schoolwork than on running a business.' Another glance across the table. 'Don't you agree, Mum?'

Of course she agreed. He knew she agreed because identical negative thoughts had jumped between them seconds earlier.

'Your dad's right, Poppykins. It would take up too much time.'

'No it wouldn't ...' Lee protested, trying to salvage his dream.

'It would,' his dad said. 'These things are much more effort than you'd imagine.'

This was disastrous, not at all how he had intended it to go. Adulation or hero worship, or at least a 'good on you, Son', were what he'd been hoping for – expecting, even. Instead, his idea was being ambushed – shot to pieces before it was able to slip into a bullet-proof vest.

'But I don't mind if it's hard work. I'll learn loads from it. Just think how much my arithmetic will improve from adding up all the money I'll make!'

He beamed his most pleading, encouraging, honest-I'm-not-thinking-of-the-money-just-my-education eyes at his mum and dad. For a second he thought his mum was wavering, but his dad stepped in to head off any change of heart.

'I'm sorry, Lee. Good idea, but no.'

'That's not fair, Dad. Mr Scales said we should get out there and do what he did – become as successful as he is.'

'But Mr Scales went to school first, Lee. It was only *after* he'd finished school that he went into business. And it was only once he was in his late thirties that he set up his own business.'

'Well, okay, so I'm a few years ahead of him ...'

Rebecca was keeping her head down – all the way to her plate, from which she was licking sauce, having already sucked up all of her spaghetti. She seemed oblivious to the devastating impact this moment could have on Lee's life; one minute an aspiring businessman with a brilliant idea, the next just another kid, his dreams lying in tatters. (The same tatters two of his comics had ended up in earlier that week after Rebecca had torn them up to make clothes for her dolls.)

'Why don't you suggest it to the school, Sugarplum. Maybe they'd be interested in setting up something for the kids.'

'Because, Mum, it's *my* idea! Why would I want to suggest it to someone else? I'd be creating competitors.'

'Not if you weren't going to be doing it yourself anyway,' Lee's dad said. 'Mum's right, be community spirited and share the idea so that everyone can benefit from it. You know, there's just not enough of that sort of thinking these days. Everyone's just thinking about how they can make a fast buck. If only they could realise that by sharing ideas the world would be a better place ...'

Lee's mum started collecting the empty dinner plates, signalling that it was pointless trying to discuss the matter any further because she wasn't going to listen ... and because Lee's dad had started waffling about politics and how the world should be run.

'Well, how about if I take Rogan for a walk?' Lee thought he might as well try now and get the bad news over with in one go.

To his surprise, his dad perked up. 'Ah, now that sounds like a much better idea, doesn't it?' he said to Lee's mum.

'Pardon?' Lee's mum said, not listening because she assumed he was still ranting.

'Lee wants to walk the dog from across the road. Sounds okay, don't you think?'

'As long as he has a lead on and sticks to the pavement. And as long as you wear a fluorescent jacket once it gets dark. And as long as they pay you a decent amount. And as long as you're back in time for your dinner. And as long as ...'

Lee's dad interrupted. 'So what your trade union official is saying, Lee, is yes, that's fine, subject to one or two reasonable conditions.'

Lee's Uncle Raymond was at the school gates on Friday. Lee's parents were going off for what they described as a 'much needed break' on their own and Uncle Raymond and his partner, Liz, had offered to look after Lee and Rebecca. Uncle Raymond had already taken Rebecca to the park while waiting for Lee's school to finish.

Lee was looking forward to the weekend. Staying at Uncle Raymond's farm was always great fun. It was out in the countryside, where everything was so different from what Lee normally experienced. You couldn't see your neighbours' houses and there wasn't a constant buzz of traffic. Then there were the country smells. Some were refreshing, though others made you want to reach for a sick-bag.

There would be loads to do, and they'd probably get to go on Uncle Raymond's new tractor.

The weekend would also provide Lee with the perfect opportunity to talk through his tuck shop idea. Uncle Raymond was a farmer, and, as he was always reminding Lee, farmers were businessmen, not just tractor drivers. Plus, Liz ran a Bed & Breakfast at the farmhouse, so she would know something about business as well. Lee was confident that he could rely on them both not to say anything to his parents if he asked them to keep it secret, which seemed the best plan given how his mum and dad had initially reacted to his idea.

It was an hour and a half's drive to the farm. The roads started off big and wide, but narrowed as they drove on.

'Why do you live in the middle of nowhere?' Rebecca asked Uncle Raymond.

Lee sniggered.

'Because that's the best place to have a farm,' Uncle Raymond explained. 'There wouldn't be enough land for a farm near a city, or if there was, it would be too expensive. People want houses near cities, not fields of potatoes, wheat and turnips.'

'Or pigs,' Lee said, remembering the time his dad had driven past a pig farm. The smell had been so bad that it had nearly put Lee off bacon for life.

Nearly, but not quite.

Uncle Raymond told them that Liz would be cooking dinner that evening. 'You'll need to have the same as the guests, mind, but I think you'll enjoy whatever she makes.'

Lee was certain he would. Liz was a brilliant cook, much better than his mum (though obviously he never told his mum that. He didn't want to have to make his own meals for the rest of his years. Anyway, it wasn't so much that his mum was a bad cook, it was more that she was disorganised. The mashed potatoes were always ready five minutes after the sausages and gravy had been served; the chips were invariably ready ten minutes before the fish; and her pizzas were usually ready seven minutes before being taken out of the oven, which was why they looked remarkably like hockey pucks. If only she could get her timing right he was sure her food would be delicious).

They were almost there. Uncle Raymond drove the Land Rover up the rough road towards the farm, between tall hedges. But from their elevated position, they were able to look out over the fields on either side.

'What are those?' Rebecca asked, pointing to where a crop of low-lying green balls were growing.

Uncle Raymond looked to see where she was indicating. 'Ah, now those are cabbages. And very tasty they are, too.'

'Yuck! I hate cabbages.'

'What! No, they're delicious. When was the last time you tried one?'

'You've never had one,' Lee told her. 'Mum doesn't like

them so she doesn't buy them for us.'

'Oh, that's right,' Uncle Raymond said. 'I'd forgotten about that. Whenever your granny served up boiled cabbage your mother would turn her nose up at it, as if someone had given her a plate of nettles.'

'Nettles sting,' Rebecca informed him.

'That's right. But they lose their sting when you cook them,' Uncle Raymond said. 'You can make nettle soup, or nettle tea.'

Rebecca wasn't convinced. 'No you can't. You're just pretending.'

'I'm not,' Uncle Raymond assured her, but Rebecca insisted she'd ask Liz to tell her the truth about nettles as soon as they arrived at the farmhouse.

Liz opened the door of the Land Rover for them. 'Hiya you two.'

'Hi,' Lee replied brightly.

Rebecca had other things on her mind. 'Uncle Raymond's silly. He says you put stingy nettles in soup.'

And so Liz had to explain that it was true, however silly it might seem.

They grabbed their bags and carried them into the house

and upstairs. 'You'll need to share a room this time,' Liz explained. 'The other rooms are all full tonight.'

Lee wasn't keen on the idea of sharing with Rebecca but decided it would be impolite to complain. Anyway, it was only for a couple of nights. He'd survive.

With their stuff dumped in a corner of their bedroom, they headed back along the landing and down the steep side staircase, the tight turns of which reminded Lee of a helter-skelter. This was the back way into the kitchen, where super-efficient Liz had set out a jug of juice ready for their arrival.

'This is such a cool place to live,' Lee declared. 'It feels like a small castle.'

'It feels like quite a big one when I'm doing the cleaning,' Liz observed. 'Now then, it'll be quite a while until we can have our dinner, so who fancies one of these to keep them going?' She reached into the fridge and brought out two slices of caramel shortcake. 'Homemade, of course.'

'Me!' Lee and Rebecca cried, like a couple of seals who've just seen the zookeeper holding a bucket of fish.

The next morning Lee awoke to the most fantastic smell wafting up from the kitchen. It was the sort of smell worth jumping out of bed for, and it meant that Liz was making her famed 'Very Full Breakfast' (as it was typed on the menus).

The Bed & Breakfast was busy. Several families had arrived the night before, keeping Liz on her toes. The guests were having to work out where they could possibly stick a mountain of eggs, sausages, bacon, black pudding, mushrooms, tomatoes, fried bread and beans, not to mention the racks of toast and piles of croissants laid out for them. They didn't stand a chance.

Meanwhile, Lee and Rebecca were in the kitchen tearing into a more manageable pile of the same food.

Liz had said she would help Rebecca with some baking once the guests had all gone. Rebecca loved baking but rarely had the chance to do it, so she was relishing the prospect. That suited Lee. He would be able to go out into the fields with Uncle Raymond, and while there he would be able to talk to him about his tuck shop idea without Rebecca listening to their every word and reporting back to their mum and dad.

It was a busy time of year for Uncle Raymond. 'Nature doesn't take weekends off,' he told Lee and Rebecca as they walked to the outbuilding where all the farm equipment was kept, 'so there's plenty I'll need to get on with while you're here. But you're welcome to tag along so long as you're careful and do as you're told. There's a lot of dangerous machinery on the farm, as I've told you before.'

Lee and Rebecca took his cautions to heart because Uncle Raymond usually joked and laughed and never seemed to take anything too seriously, so they knew to take heed when he did say something was important.

'Will you still be able to play with us?' Rebecca wanted to know.

'I'll play as much as I can. I'm just saying that I have to work non-stop at this time of year. If I don't, then I won't get the quality of crops that I want. Or the yield, for that matter.'

'What's the yield?' Lee asked.

'It's where they grow things,' Rebecca stated proudly.

'Ha ha. No, that's the field,' Uncle Raymond explained.

'The yield is how much you get out of each field. The aim is to get as high a yield as possible to make the best use of the land you've bought and all the equipment you've used for harvesting the crops.'

Rebecca was bewildered by this explanation, so she tried

a different tact.

'How do people become farmers?'

'Oh, some are born into it – their parents have a farm and they work on it with them, then take it over when their parents retire. Others decide it's what they want to do, so they go to college, then work on someone else's farm until they're ready to buy their own.'

'You took over from Great Uncle Desmond, didn't you?' Lee asked.

'That's right. I used to spend every summer helping him here, learning what needed to be done. And then, not long before he popped his clogs, I bought the farm from him.'

After a tour of the outbuildings they headed back to the farmhouse. The guests were packing up for their day out and about in the countryside and Liz was making sure they all had the packed lunches she'd made for them. Uncle Raymond led Lee and Rebecca inside and sat them at the kitchen table while he made a cup of tea.

'Do you like being a farmer?' Lee asked.

'It has good and bad points,' Uncle Raymond told him, but didn't elaborate on what they were, so in his head Lee drew a chart comparing his dad's life as a businessman with Uncle Raymond's life as a farmer.

Category	Uncle Raymond
Getting to work	Already there
Surroundings at work	In the middle of the beautiful countryside
Social life	None—presumably that's why he invited Liz to live with him
Hours of work	Long
Money earned	Not all that much judging from his clothes
Car driven	A 4X4 that other people move out of the way for
Boss	None – he's his own boss, with no-one else to nag him
Holidays	Not many – nature stops for no man
Stress	None, apparently, because Uncle Raymond is always in a good mood
Neighbours	Half a mile to the nearest ones, which is rubbish if you are a kid and want someone to play with, and is a long way to go to borrow a screwdriver

Dad	Winner
Has to fight his way through massive traffic jams or catch the train	Uncle Raymond
In a concrete office block	Uncle Raymond
Lots of colleagues and lots of after-work drinks	Dad
Long	Draw
Not all that much judging from what's left over for my pocket money	Draw
A family saloon that would be crushed by the 4X4 in a battle	Uncle Raymond
The fabulously inspirational Mr Wayne Scales	Sort of a draw in a way
Five weeks a year	Dad
Lots, because Dad has bags under his eyes and wrinkles on his forehead	Uncle Raymond
Six inches to Holly Arthanthou, if you drilled through the wall; otherwise twenty metres if you went up the path, out the gate and then down her front path	Uncle Raymond

Adding it up with those criteria it worked out at a draw, but Lee couldn't help thinking that, on balance, Uncle Raymond had a better life.

Liz returned to the kitchen. 'Well, that's the guests all off. Just the rooms to clean and then, Rebecca, we can get baking.'

'Yippee!'

'Have a cup of tea first,' Uncle Raymond insisted to Liz, easing her into a seat. To Lee and Rebecca he said, 'She's a hardworking woman is my Liz.'

Uncle Raymond wasn't joking. Liz got up at six in the morning, a time Lee had only heard of. She made breakfast for up to fifteen people and, while she was doing that, also made packed lunches for them if they wanted to have a picnic out in the countryside; she then cleaned all the rooms, made Uncle Raymond's lunch, went to the shops for supplies and was back by late afternoon, just in time to welcome more guests. She would show them to their rooms and, because her cooking was renowned, more often than not she'd be asked to make dinner for them, so she'd make it, serve it (though Uncle Raymond often helped out with that part), then do all the dishes afterwards. Wonder Woman was lazy in comparison to Liz. All Wonder Woman had to do was occasionally save the human race from a supervillain.

Uncle Raymond poured Liz's tea and she gulped it down as if she didn't have enough time to savour it properly. Which she clearly didn't, because a minute later she bounded off with Rebecca to tidy the bedrooms.

That left Lee to head down to the fields with Uncle Raymond.

This was the moment Lee had been waiting for. They were barely out of the door before he was setting out his plans for a mobile tuck shop and explaining his parents' opposition to the idea.

Uncle Raymond listened carefully, nodding every so often and making 'uh huh' noises.

'So what do you think I should do?' Lee eventually asked. 'Should I forget the whole idea, like Mum and Dad say, or should I go for it regardless?'

'Hmmm. That's an awkward one. You don't want to go against your mum and dad, do you? And yet there's something bigger at stake than whether or not you're going to do as you're told.'

'You bet. I've got my business empire to think about. This could be the major leap forward I've been looking for, something more than just washing cars, tidying gardens and walking dogs.'

'You know, Lee, Rome wasn't built in a day,' Uncle Raymond said profoundly.

'How long did it take, then?'

'I've no idea, but the point is that it wasn't built in a day. Do you understand what I'm saying? Small steps get you there just the same as big ones.'

Lee kind of understood. 'Don't rush things, is that what you mean?'

'That's it. Sometimes it's better to do the right thing eventually than to do the wrong thing simply because you lack patience.'

They walked on silently until they reached the gate to the nearest field to the farmhouse.

'So you don't think I should do it,' Lee said, trying to keep disappointment from his voice.

'Tell me this: how much do you think you could make from running this mobile tuck shop?'

'I don't really know ...'

'And what would you sell?'

'Sweets.'

'What kind?'

'Well ...'

'And how much would you sell them for? The same as the local shops? Less? More?'

'I haven't decided yet ...'

'Lee, I'm not saying don't do it; I'm saying do it properly. What would you say to me if I planted a field full of something it turned out nobody wanted?'

'Well ...'

'Go on, now. Tell me straight.'

'Well, okay. I'd say you were a real idiot.'

'Eh, yes. Or words to that effect. Yeah, and you'd be right, I would be an idiot. Why didn't I find out what people wanted before I started sowing, eh?' Uncle Raymond put a hand on Lee's shoulder. 'Well it's the same for you. Find out what your customers want before you start a business. And work out if you can actually make money from it.'

'But what about Mum and Dad?'

Uncle Raymond looked out across his field. 'When Bill Gates set up Microsoft, I'll bet his mum and dad said, "Bill, that Microsoft computer software of yours will never take off. Just get a job in the hardware store like everyone else." But he was prepared to take a chance. And now look at him. He's one of the wealthiest men on the planet!'

'Richer than Wayne Scales – Dad's boss?'

'Much richer.'

'Wow!'

'Bill Gates is worth more than some countries.'

'Which ones?'

'I don't know. The smaller ones, I guess.'

'Why doesn't he buy one, then?'

Uncle Raymond thought about this, then said, 'I guess most countries aren't for sale.'

They tramped across the field, walking between the rows of young potato plants.

'Are you rich?' Lee asked his uncle.

'Me? No, I'm a farmer.'

'Farmers are allowed to be rich, aren't they?'

'Oh sure. But they're not allowed to admit it.'

'Is that why they drive around in old cars and wear tatty clothes?'

'That's it. We don't want the secret to get out.'

A man in a flat cap called to them from the gate at the other end of the field, raising his arm in a wave at the same time. Lee couldn't work out what the man had said, but Uncle Raymond obviously could and called back hello. 'That's Colin Flower,' he told Lee. 'Or Cawly, as everyone knows him. He owns the farm to the north of ours. Minted, he is.'

'Really?'

'Worth an absolute fortune.'

Lee looked again at Cawly Flower, trying not to stare. 'He

doesn't look it,' he told Uncle Raymond. 'Not by a long shot.'

'He's like every other farmer. His fortune's tied up in his land.'

'Why doesn't he sell it then?'

'Because what use is a farmer without land? A man without land isn't a farmer, is he?'

'Can't you rent land from someone else?'

'You can. But most of the time it's not what's in the ground that's valuable, it's the ground that it's in.'

On the way back to the farmhouse, Uncle Raymond taught Lee to ask himself an important question, namely: What's the downside?

At first Lee didn't understand what this meant, but Uncle Raymond soon explained. 'What's the worst that can happen? If your business going wrong would be a major financial disaster, then you need to think twice about starting it, but if the worst would be that you didn't sell much and were left with some sweets under your bed or wherever ... Well, that would hardly be the end of the world, would it?'

'I suppose not.'

'You might lose a few quid in the process, but you could write that off as the price of experience. Nothing ventured, nothing gained, as the old saying goes. Just don't bet your granny on it.'

'I wasn't going to. How would I explain it to Mum and Dad if I lost?'

'Eh, that's just an expression, Lee.'

'Aw. Right. I thought you meant ... Never mind.'

With Uncle Raymond now on his side, Lee's confidence returned. Of course he should go for it with the mobile tuck shop! As Uncle Raymond said, there were always people queuing up to tell you why you shouldn't be doing something, but where were they when you made a success of it? First in the queue to ask for your autograph.

So while Liz was making dinner and Uncle Raymond was having a bath, Lee practised writing out his name to ensure he would be able to sign with a flurry.

By that night Lee had sorted out quite a few details of how he would run his business. But one crucial problem remained: where could he store his stock?

This was bothering Lee. He couldn't put it under his bed because Rebecca would probably find it and scoff the lot. But where else was there?

He raised the issue with Uncle Raymond, but all he said

was, 'Hmmm, yes, that's a thought'. And so when they sat down for dinner at eight o'clock Lee still hadn't come up with a solution.

They were eating long past Rebecca's bedtime and normally she would have been unbearably grumpy because of it, but Liz had promised they could devour one of the cakes she had helped to make, so Rebecca remained bright and cheery, desperate to taste it and find out what everyone else thought of her creation.

Liz wanted to know everything that had happened to Lee and Rebecca since she'd last seen them. How was school? How was nursery? How were the teachers? How was the homework? Did Lee have any girlfriends? (How embarrassing.) Did Rebecca have any boyfriends? (Three, so she claimed!)

'So, has your dad started doing anything about that mess at the bottom of your garden? He's always saying he's going to, but never seems to get round to it.'

'No ...' Lee said, and even before he'd finished saying that one word an idea was already forming in his head, an idea that would instantly solve the problem of storing his stock.

'And now, Ladies and Gentlemen, to open your new store

– the one hundredth in the country – I give you your company's chief executive ...' The cheering was starting already. '... The one and only ... the amazing ... Lee Waters!' Now the crowd was ecstatic. But Lee was modest. Fame hadn't gone to his head.

It had, however, gone to his clothing, because he was dressed in a snazzy outfit. Not the grey suit, shirt and tie that successful businessmen normally wore, instead he was wearing baggy jeans and a cool red sweatshirt with *Tuck In* emblazoned across the front in large gold letters.

It took quite a while to quieten the enthusiastic crowd, but eventually Lee was able to make himself heard using a microphone.

'Thank you, thank you. I am delighted to be here today to mark the opening of this, our one-hundredth store. This is an important milestone for our company. We started out just two years ago with me carrying a few bars of chocolate to school in my clapped out old schoolbag, and now look how far we've come! Pupils all around the country can now take advantage of *Tuck In*. Some buy from our in-school representatives, while many others buy after school and at weekends by flocking to *Tuck In* stores like the one we're opening today.

'Of course, becoming this successful hasn't been easy.

It's taken a lot of hard work and, because of that, I've flunked occasional tests at school, like the Maths one last week, which was murder. But it's been my willingness to make those sorts of sacrifices that has brought me this far. What's one crummy Maths test compared to the creation of an entire business empire? I may not be a Maths genius, but I can still count the number of swimming pools in my mansions. For that matter, I can still count the number of countries in which I own mansions. But the point is, we're here, we've made it happen and we're going to keep on making it happen!'

The crowd cheered. 'Open! Open!' they chanted, and so Lee picked up the golden scissors, held them out to the tape and …

'Lee, that's breakfast ready.'

'Hang on a second, I'm just cutting the tape.'

'You're what?'

'Eh?'

Uncle Raymond was standing at the bedroom door, confused.

Lee rubbed his eyes. 'Oh, right, I'm eh, just, well, getting up for one of Liz's delicious breakfasts.'

'Okay, Sleepyhead, I'll see you downstairs in a minute.'

Like his dad, Lee took a good five minutes to become

65

vaguely human after a good, long sleep, whereas Rebecca was instantly full of energy. It was as if she could only ever be completely on or completely off, nothing in between. So, while she leapt out of bed and charged off towards the kitchen, Lee slowly rolled out, sighed, picked himself up off the floor he'd rolled out onto and thought about dressing.

It was only after he'd spent a full minute looking for his *Tuck In* sweatshirt that he realised he'd been dreaming.

Still, his dream was inspirational, and as soon as Uncle Raymond dropped him and Rebecca home, Lee tore upstairs to his bedroom with only a 'Hi' to his parents at the door on the way past. If he was going to become as successful as his dream had suggested, then he'd better get on with selling those old toys he had stacked up so neatly in his bedroom. He needed the money to start his business.

'Hello, Lee!' his mum shouted upstairs. 'Nice to see you. Did you have a great weekend away, Mum and Dad? Yes, we did, thanks very much. And what about you, Lee? Did you have a good time on the farm? Oh, yes, Mum, it was great, and it was really good of Uncle Raymond and Liz to have had us over to stay. I'll just come back downstairs right now and tell Uncle Raymond how much I appreciate all the effort he and Liz went to. Oh, and while I'm there I'll actually speak more than a word to you and Dad about your own weekend to find out if you had a good time!'

Lee's mum had a talent for sarcasm, and practised regularly to maintain her skill.

'He's a young man in a hurry, that one,' Uncle Raymond

told her. 'A head full of great ideas.'

'He's enthusiastic, I'll give you that.'

'He's certainly keen on the idea of a yard sale,' Uncle Raymond informed her. 'Hasn't stopped talking about it the whole time he's been with us. Has it all thought through.'

The adults had moved to the kitchen by now, where Lee's mum was making Uncle Raymond a cuppa and telling him all about the wonderful walks she and Lee's dad had been on, and about all the wonderful buildings they'd seen. Lee sat listening at the top of the stairs, impressed that Uncle Raymond had managed to encourage the idea of the yard sale even before he'd stepped through the front door. It was all going even better than the two of them had planned back at the farm.

And so, five days later, at 2.00pm on Saturday afternoon (and after Lee had washed Holly Arthanthou's car earlier that morning), Lee officially opened his yard sale. The queue went all the way back to the open front gate, although that wasn't very far given as it was also where the queue started.

Or, to put it another way, there was only one person in

the queue.

That one person was Will, who'd promised to help Lee man the stall.

'Can't I come in now?' Will asked.

'No, I need you to stand outside and make it look busy.'

Will looked around. 'How can I make it look busy if I'm on my own?'

'Well at least if you're there people will be able to see where the sale is.'

Will wasn't convinced, but nonetheless stood at the gate, trying to look like he was eager to get to the tables of old toys that Lee had set up in the driveway.

Ten minutes later, still no-one had arrived. After fifteen minutes he said, 'This isn't going to work, is it?'

Lee was bitterly disappointed. 'I can't understand it. If I'd seen one of my posters, I'd be first in the queue.'

For something to do, Will wandered over to the nearest lamppost to read what Lee had attached to it.

'Hang on!' he called over a few seconds later. 'Your posters say the sale starts at two-thirty, not two o'clock!'

Lee came alive again, like a vampire after drinking a few pints of blood. 'Do they?' He stepped out of the driveway to have a look for himself. 'Oh man! That's right! I was going to have it at two o'clock but I didn't think I'd have finished washing Holly's car and getting everything ready by then, so I moved it back!'

'No wonder there's no-one ....' Will let his words trail off because he could see a group of five young kids approaching up the hill. They were walking quickly, as if they were worried they might miss out on something. 'Do you think maybe ...?'

Lee tried to suppress a grin, but it didn't co-operate and instead wrapped itself all the way round his face, making him look like a human postbox.

'I hope so.'

It didn't take the kids long to arrive at Lee's gate, where Will quickly made it look as if there was no way he was going to give up his position at the front of the queue.

'Is this the right house for the Trash For Cash sale?' asked a boy of about eight with hair so short it would be years before he next needed to visit a barber.

Will was about to say it was when Lee intervened. 'No, this is a Yard Sale, like it says on the poster I put up. There's no trash for sale here, only quality merchandise at fantastic value-for-money prices.' It was what he'd heard someone say on the radio.

'Great,' the kid said. 'My mum said it would just be a load of old rubbish.'

'Not at all. And I'll tell you what, as you lot are first to arrive, I'll allow you in early to have a sneak preview.'

'Cool.'

The five kids started picking up and inspecting everything that Lee had laid out so carefully. Lee was just about to put the items back neatly when one of the kids yelled, 'Look! Lego!' The others quickly huddled around, rummaging through everything they could lay their hands on. 'Wow, it's the jungle adventure series!' someone cried. 'Cool!'

'How much for this?' a blonde kid asked, holding up a Lego jungle jeep as if were the World Cup.

'It's ... actually, I can't sell it to you right now because it's not official opening time yet.'

'Okay, how much *will* it be?'

Lee hadn't decided what he'd charge for anything because he wasn't sure how much people would be prepared to pay. 'Two pounds,' he said confidently, having no idea if that was way too much or an out and out bargain.

'Two pounds!'

'Yes. Although someone else might offer more. I suppose that's the chance you'll have to take. Buy it now for that bargain price or hold off, and then someone else will snap it up.'

'Oh yeah? Like who?'

'Like one of those people coming up the road.'

The kid turned around and saw a group of ten adults and children heading in the direction of Lee's house. He hummed and hawed, trying to decide what to do, so Lee picked up the jungle jeep, held it above his head and yelled, 'Mint condition Lego jungle jeep for sale! Who else wants it?'

The blonde boy panicked, worried that someone else might arrive and outbid him for the item he had now set his heart on. 'Okay, okay. I'll take it for two pounds,' he blurted out.

'Excellent,' Lee said. 'I think you've made a good decision. I could probably have got a lot more for it if I'd wanted.'

The kid handed over his cash before Lee changed his mind, not knowing that that was about as likely as Lee volunteering to sit through extra school lessons at weekends.

Lee was amazed and delighted that he'd been able to get away with charging two pounds for a jeep that had a couple of bits missing and no instructions. It was great to know there were plenty of suckers out there, and even better to know that right at that moment they were holding their annual convention in his family's driveway.

The group of ten people reached Lee's gate.

And walked right past it.

As Lee dropped the two-pound coin into his trouser pocket, he started to consider what else he could flog to these kids. 'Do any of you like Action Man?' he asked.

'Me!' cried a lad with most of his lunch still stuck to his T-shirt.

'Me, too,' called the tallest of the kids, who was wearing training shoes so large that they must have been built in a shipyard.

'Well,' Lee responded, 'I've got some Action Man gear that I wasn't really planning on selling ... but I suppose ... well, I could let you see it ...'

'What sort of gear?' he was asked.

'Tanks, boats, equipment ... Is it worth my while going to the effort of digging it out?'

'Yeah, I might buy some if you let us see it.'

'It's all really good quality as well ...' Lee continued.

'Show us it!' all the kids clamoured.

'I don't know ...'

'Go on!'

'Oh well, okay then,' Lee said, as if the notion of selling these new items was tugging hard at his heart strings. Lee asked Will to watch the stall to make sure his old toys didn't all disappear without being paid for, then stepped into the house and grabbed a box that was already sitting at the bottom of the stairs. Looking at the Action Man gear he realised he should have given it away years ago. He was way too old for it now. It was embarrassing even admitting he still had it.

'That was quick,' a boy said when Lee reappeared two seconds later. 'I thought they were buried away somewhere.'

'No, no, they were very close at hand because...I play with them all the time.' Lee ignored the quizzical look Will threw him and carried on. 'They're probably my favourite toys out of everything I own. Will is always asking to borrow them overnight, but I never let him, they're too precious to me.'

'I don't ...' Will began.

'Get them,' Lee finished for him. 'No, that's right.'

'So are they expensive?' asked the boy.

'Why, do you like them?' Lee asked.

'Sure.'

'Well, okay. I'll tell you what. Seeing as you're a big Action Man fan, just like me, I'll let you have them for a good bit less than they're worth, because I believe these are becoming collectors items and are selling for huge amounts in auctions.'

'If that's the case,' the blonde kid said, 'why are you selling them cheap to us instead of taking them to an auction company?'

'Ah, now, eh the reason I'm not doing that is because...I happen to think it's very important that these toys find a home where they will be cherished just as they have been in my home. Somewhere they'll give another kid just as much pleasure and enjoyment as they've given me over the years. You're right, I could sell them for a fortune at auction, but when it comes to these toys it's not money that's important to me.'

'How much for the boat then?'

'Ten pounds.'

'Ten pounds! You're kidding! I'll give you five.'

'Nine pound fifty.'

'Six.'

'Okay, nine pound fifty-six.'

'No, I meant six pounds.'

'Okay, nine pound forty.'

'You're supposed to go down by the same amount as I go up,' the kid told Lee.

'Okay, what are you going to then?'

'Seven pounds.'

'Nine pound thirty.'

'What! Forget it.'

'Okay, okay. It's just that this stuff is so valuable to me that I don't want to lose it.'

'Why are you selling it then?'

'Eh, I have to.'

'Why? Won't your parents let you keep it in your room?'

'No, it's ... well, you see, my pet dog is desperately sick and I'm trying to raise money so he can have an operation that might just save his life.'

'That's terrible,' said a quiet young lad who had been going through a box of old books. 'I've got a dog and I'd do anything to save him. I think it's really good that you're prepared to sacrifice your toys for him. Here, I'll buy these two books. This one looks particularly good'. He held it up. *Lee and the Consul Mutants*, the title read.

'That's one of the best books I've ever read,' Lee told the kid. 'You should definitely take that one. You'll love it. I can't recommend it highly enough.'

'Really? Sounds great. How much?'

'How much have you got with you?'

'A fiver.'

'Well that's a stroke of luck, because that's how much it costs.'

'A fiver! That's almost as much as it costs new. And this one's second hand.'

Lee rearranged his facial muscles so it seemed as if he was about to burst into tears. 'I'm only thinking of my poor dog. Vets charge so much these days that I'm not sure I'm going to be able to afford to have his life saved ...'

'Oh well, I suppose if it's for your dog ...' The kid handed over all the money he had with him.

As Lee pocketed the cash, the kid said, 'Where is your dog? Can I see him?'

'Ah...no, sadly not. The vet said that the excitement of meeting someone new might well kill him.'

'Why, is he a really shy vet?'

And so it went on into the afternoon, with Lee fleecing as much money as possible from each and every customer, telling them whatever story they wanted to hear in order to part them from their cash.

With his trouser pockets heavy with the stash of cash he'd raised from his yard sale, Lee luckily only had to wait another week before Uncle Raymond would be visiting again. In the meantime, he decided that some market research was required before he set up his new business. So he headed off to the local shop, where kids spent their pocket money on the way to and from school.

The shop was owned by a man whom all the kids called Panface. He looked as if he'd lost an argument with the sort of heavy frying pan that could cook eight eggs at once with room to spare for several slices of fried bread. Thus his name. Panface wasn't a nice name, but then Panface wasn't a nice man, so they were well suited.

Lee's mum tried to avoid using Panface's shop. (Yes, even she called him that.) Only in absolute emergencies would she allow any member of her family (which usually meant Lee) to enter it. Panface gave her the creeps. She reckoned that he looked at people in a weird way, as if he were a cannibal trying to decide how long he'd need to cook them for before eating them for lunch with a healthy side salad.

Plus, most of what he sold was probably older than Lee's grannies and cost more than either of them were ever likely to leave in their wills. According to Lee's mum, Panface only survived in business because local people had nowhere else to go unless they wanted to drive to the supermarket.

So although Lee was less than enthusiastic about entering Panface's shop, he knew he needed to check out the competition. Perhaps he would be able to spot new opportunities for making a fortune and becoming the world's richest boy.

The shop door squeaked a little as Lee entered, but there wasn't the ding that normally greeted customers. Panface was nowhere to be seen.

Lee took advantage of this situation. He closed the door as quietly as he could, letting go of the edge just before his fingers got crushed, then tip-toed behind the shelf in the middle, confident that he wouldn't be seen if he hid there behind the loaves of bread and packets of sugar.

He was able to study Panface's shop, soaking up valu - able information. Lee had never before paid attention to the way shops were laid out, but now he saw that the cheap sweets were at the front where the kids could reach them, and the more expensive ones were at the back, presumably because they were most likely to be bought by adults, who had longer arms and deeper pockets. And with the comics, the key was to make sure the titles could be seen clearly. Lee stored away this observation at the back of his mind – a place where there was plenty of unused space.

'Can I get you something?'

Lee hadn't heard Panface leave the back room of the shop and nearly jumped out of his skin when he turned to find the unfortunate-looking shopkeeper at his shoulder. (Fortunately Lee had zipped his skin up nice and tight earlier that morning, so he didn't embarrass himself.)

Panface had eventually detected the presence of a customer in his shop and, like a tarantula scuttling towards prey in its web, had set out to investigate.

Lee regained his composure. 'Eh, no thanks. I was just having a look to see what I could spend next week's pocket money on.'

'Forward planning?'

'Eh, uh-huh.'

'There's no law against that,' Panface declared. 'Not yet,' he added threateningly. 'So, has anything caught your eye? Anything edible? Anything educational? Anything entertaining?'

'Not really.'

This wasn't the answer Panface had been hoping for. 'Oh. Well maybe it's best to earn it before you spend it.'

Lee wandered over to the corner, all the time pretending to look at the stock on the shelves when what he was really interested in was the small store room at the rear of the shop where Panface had been lurking, waiting to pounce. It was possible to see into it if you stood near the rack of comics, so Lee picked one up at random and looked over the top of it. Behind him, Panface rearranged some tins, then retreated to his counter.

In the store room, boxes were stacked on top of each other as if Panface had spent the day building towers. Most of the boxes contained sweets, and Lee could just about read the numbers on the side. 24 bars; 36 bars; some even contained 48 bars. That was more bars than the average prison cell.

'Hi, Lee,' someone said to him from behind.

The voice was too young to be Panface's. Lee spun round to see whose it was.

It belonged to Craig, one of Lee's classmates and a creep of the highest order. Craig was forever acting like Mr Cool, going around saying things like, 'Hey man,' and 'What's up, Dude?' and 'Cosmic'. He would have been an object of ridicule were it not for the fact that he'd been born with more muscles than most wrestlers and didn't mind who he used them to bully.

'Hey Dude, interesting comic you've got there.'

Lee hadn't bothered to check which comic he'd picked up, he'd just grabbed the one that was closest, his attention focused entirely on the contents of the room at the back of the shop. Now he looked at the front cover and saw that he was holding a copy of *Jackie*.

'Looks like you're reading it pretty closely, Man,' Craig mocked. 'Stories good, are they? Right up your street?'

'Eh, my little sister wanted me to make sure it had a...' Lee looked at the page again in desperation, '... a Jane's Farm story in it before I bought it for her.'

'And has it?'

'Eh, yeah.'

'Lucky little sister, then.'

Lee tried to smile as if he were happy for Rebecca.

Craig leaned forward on the balls of his feet. 'So aren't you going to get it for her?' he asked, eyebrows raised to reveal that even they were controlled by bulging muscles. 'She'll be keen to read it as soon as possible if it's her favourite.'

'Eh ...' Lee stuck a hand in his pocket and pulled out all

the money he had with him. 'Oh heck,' he said. 'She hasn't given me enough money! What a shame. She'll be so disappointed.'

'No problem. Mum only had a two-pound coin and my comic's just seventy pence. I'll lend you the rest and you can give me it back at school. I'm sure Mum won't mind.'

What was Lee to do? There seemed to be no way out. If he didn't accept Craig's offer of a loan then word would soon be round his classmates that he'd been caught reading a girl's comic at Panface's shop. But if he went ahead and bought it, on the pretence that it was for Rebecca (even if she was far too young to read it), that would mean wasting his own money on a girls' comic!

'Hang on,' Lee said, suddenly coming up with an idea. He looked at the front cover of the comic again. 'Oh no! It's the one she's already got. She'll be gutted.'

'Yeah, sure,' Craig said. 'Cosmically devastated, I'll bet.'

Lee made for the counter, where he picked up the nearest bar of chocolate and handed his money to Panface, who took it without saying a word. Seconds later Lee was heading for the shop's tatty door.

Except that before he reached it he heard a cough. A woman's cough. And it came from the shop's store room. In other circumstances he might have stopped, spun around and investigated. As it was, he carried on without breaking his stride, mightily relieved to be leaving with his pride just about intact.

A week later a fictitious visit to the nearby Transport Museum provided the perfect excuse for Lee and Uncle Raymond to visit a cash and carry. It was Lee's chance to buy the initial stock for his mobile tuck shop.

Uncle Raymond usually wore the worst clothes in the world – clothes almost as filthy and smelly as those worn by The Rat, the music teacher at Lee's school. However, fortunately he'd tidied up for their trip to civilisation.

'Here we go,' Uncle Raymond said.

From the outside it looked like ... well, like a warehouse, neither interesting nor attractive. Lee had been expecting an especially fancy supermarket, one that sold products you couldn't buy anywhere else.

'This is it?' he checked, though he doubted Uncle Raymond would have taken him to the wrong place.

'Ah,' Uncle Raymond said, realising Lee's disappointment. 'I know what you're thinking. But just wait 'til you get inside.'

And he was right.

'Wow!' Lee cried as he stood at the door and peered past

the man who was checking Uncle Raymond's membership card.

It was a serious 'wow', because as Lee looked up the first few aisles he realised he'd never before seen so much food packed in such large quantities. Everything was either in a giant packet or came in tens, fifties or hundreds, when normally ones or twos would do.

'This place is amazing!'

Uncle Raymond had a list of items Liz had asked him to buy for the Bed & Breakfast. 'Now then,' he said as they stood at the end of a wide aisle, 'toilet rolls.'

When they found them Lee discovered that you couldn't buy the sort of pack that his mum bought – nine rolls, maybe twelve if there was a special offer on – no, the packs in the warehouse contained about one hundred rolls! That was a lot of snot and ...

Lee didn't really want to think about what else it was a lot of.

Uncle Raymond placed the enormous bag of toilet rolls on the rack under their trolley, and carried on. Their trolley was three times the size of one in normal supermarkets, but then it needed to be; soon they had it half-filled with giant trays of croissants and slabs of butter bigger than bricks. Lee reckoned it was as well Uncle Raymond was used to driving tractors, because their trolley was almost as big and heavy as one.

'Right, that's me got everything for Liz,' Uncle Raymond said eventually, 'so let's see about your stuff.' And they headed for the aisles that were piled to the ceiling with bags of crisps and packets of sweets.

It wasn't easy for Lee to distract his mum and dad long enough to unload his stock, but Uncle Raymond saved the day by developing a passionate desire to find an old photograph he was suddenly convinced was somewhere in the front room of Lee's parents' house. While Lee's mum and dad pulled the room apart trying to uncover the photo, Lee opened the back of Uncle Raymond's Land Rover and grabbed some of the boxes sitting on the floor.

Uncle Raymond, who seemed to think he'd become the commander in an army, directed the operation.

'Right, the coast's clear!' he whispered to Lee outside the front door. 'Go! Go! Go!'

Lee struggled down the driveway with as many boxes as he could carry. The boxes were heavy, but if he were to take only one at a time, he'd be there until sunrise the next morning, so he did his best, even though it meant having to walk like a penguin.

When he reached the rear of the house, he carried on down the full length of the back garden to the greenhouse.

The greenhouse must once have been the pride and joy of the house's previous owner, but for years now (basically, ever since Lee's family had moved in) it had been a mess. And Liz was right; for as long as anyone could remember, Lee's dad had been threatening to do something about tidying it up, without ever actually doing so. Still, Lee wasn't complaining – it was the one place he could put things and guarantee they would never be found. He tucked box after box under the shelves so they wouldn't be visible from the house or when anyone wandered around the garden.

One of the advantages of using the greenhouse to store his stock was that it could be accessed from a nearby gate. Both the gate and the greenhouse were hidden from the house by a huge sycamore tree that Lee's dad kept talking about cutting down. But, as with the greenhouse, he hadn't got round to sorting that out either. With the presence of the tree, Lee had worked out that, after leaving for school each morning and waving to his mum and Rebecca at the door, he could walk round the corner, nip down the back lane, enter the garden through the back gate, load up with stock for the day and, within a couple of minutes, be on his way to school.

Lee arrived back at the front door of the house after his fifth hurried trip, just in time to hear his mother shout, 'Found it!'

Lee's arms ached from carrying the boxes, and he was sweating profusely.

'Wipe your forehead and try to cool down,' Uncle Raymond advised. 'I'll try to hold them off for a few seconds longer while you make your last run.' So saying, he went inside and made a big show of his appreciation for the effort Lee's mum and dad had made to find the photograph that in truth was of no interest to him whatsoever.

Lee grabbed a last armful of boxes and waddled down the drive.

Having made a perfect job of stalling Lee's parents, Uncle Raymond stepped outside again. Lee was attempting to return his face to its normal colour following all his exertions.

Uncle Raymond winked at Lee as he prepared to leave. 'Good luck,' he said quietly. 'And let me know how you get on.'

'I will,' Lee promised.

Lee's mum moved closer. 'What are you two whispering

about?'

'Oh we're just plotting the overthrow of the government,' Uncle Raymond said.

'And the Queen,' Lee added to please his dad.

'Good on you, Son. Don't forget to take all of her possessions into public ownership, because they belong to the people of this country, not that bunch of ...'

Uncle Raymond raised his eyebrows and made a he-doesn't-half-go-on-about-this-sort-of-stuff-doesn't-he face. Then he punched a fist into the air and cried, 'Power to the people!'

Lee tried not to giggle, but the sound sneaked out through a gap between his front teeth. With it came a fine spray of mouth juices that he hadn't meant to let out but which ended up on Uncle Raymond's trousers.

Oops.

Fortunately Uncle Raymond didn't seem to notice, or if he did he ignored it. Maybe he was used to that sort of thing, Lee considered. All that gunge on the farm ....

Lee realised he should have paid more attention in mind-numbing Maths. Calculators were fine, but they weren't much use if you didn't know what you were supposed to be adding, subtracting, multiplying or dividing in the first place.

His head was buzzing with business questions, such as:

If a boy buys a box of 48 chocolate bars for £12.48, a jar of 200 chews for £1.86 and a box of 36 packets of crisps for £3.99 and takes them to school to run a mobile tuck shop:

a) How much does he need to sell each bar, packet or chew for to make a profit?

b) How much will Panface be selling them for in his shop?

c) How many bars will he sell each day?

d) How many bars can he fit in a normal schoolbag without the teachers noticing what he's up to?

e) How many bars does he need to sell before he can

buy a very large house with an enormous indoor swimming pool that he can invite all his friends round to use?

f) Oh yeah, and which friends would those be exactly?

The answer to f) was easy – they were the friends who would flock to him like bees to honey once he'd made all his millions. (Hopefully they wouldn't be like wasps buzzing expectantly to a water-filled jam jar, because that would mean his friends would all drown.) It was the other questions that were more difficult.

But then who said running a business would be easy? No-one. So he knuckled down and got on with it, making educated guesses if he didn't know answers or couldn't find them out.

After a few hours he was feeling more confident.

Having formed a better idea of how he was going to organise and run his tuck shop empire, Lee decided upon a few important ground rules.

It was important to have rules. Without them a business venture could be thrown into the sort of chaos that normally reigned in the cupboards of Lee's bedroom.

LEE'S TUCK SHOP RULES

1. Don't eat all the stock yourself.
2. Sell everything for as much as possible, even if someone pleads poverty.
3. Don't give customers anything until they've paid for it, otherwise you'll probably never see them or your stock again.
4. A desperate customer (someone who's starving) is a good customer because you can charge them more than usual.
5. Keep extra stock for your regulars. (For example, store it in a separate pocket of your schoolbag.) Regulars won't be regulars for long if you regularly don't have anything left for them when they regularly want it.
6. Be nice to your customers, they're the ones giving you the money.

Lee had decided on rule one after being tempted to open a few boxes of sweets in order to 'test' the merchandise for himself, just in case it wasn't up to scratch. Lee knew what he was like when it came to sweets: once he started he would never be able to stop, so the only answer was not to start in the first place.

There were a few potential customers to whom rule six wouldn't necessarily apply, including Craig the Creepoid. Lee couldn't imagine himself being nice to Craig under any circumstance.

Overall, these were hard-nosed, give-no-quarter, I'm-the-boss-and-don't-you-forget-it rules. And they were the rules that would make Lee successful when other, less disciplined businessmen would fail.

The Ogre was, as usual, having a right old whinge about this, that and the next thing. And a few other things besides. It was one of those days when no-one seemed able to do anything right. Especially Lee.

The Ogre moaned when he asked the girl next to him a question about the Maths exercise they were doing. (Wasn't group work supposed to be a good thing?) The Ogre huffed and puffed when he accidentally knocked his pens and pencils off the desk, scattering them over the floor. And she got in a terrible strop when Lee leaned back too far in his chair and fell over (when she should have been worried about whether he'd broken his back and needed hospital treatment).

Lee related all this to Will when they met at lunchtime.

'Most people whinge less in their entire lives than The Ogre does in half a day. She's terrible. I'll bet if she entered a Winning Whinge competition she'd win first prize easily.

No-one would bother entering against her because they wouldn't stand a chance.'

'I've got an idea,' Will said. 'Why don't you get everyone in the class to save up their pocket money and then you can buy her a round bed.'

'A round bed?' Lee queried.

'So she can't get out the wrong side in the morning.'

Lee sniggered. 'Good idea!'

'Of course,' Will went on, 'what they should really do is sack her ...'

'Too right.'

'... And then hang her.'

'You're dead right,' Lee said, not really listening to what Will was saying.

'... And then chop her up into little bits ...'

'That too.'

'... And then arrange all the little bits over the playground in the shape of an ogre and let the birds eat them ...'

'Eh, what? Eh, no, no, I think that would be taking things a bit too far.'

'You think?'

'Yeah. It'd make a mess of the playground. Leave it at chopping her up into little pieces. Maybe the zoo could feed them to the lions and tigers.'

'Do you think the zoo might take her as she is? She could be the world's first ogre in captivity!'

Lee continued to munch on his lunch. He was having a hotdog, of course. By his counting, that was now six hundred and thirty-eight school days in a row that he'd had hotdogs and he was sure that must be a record. Sometimes he fancied eating something different for lunch, just for a change, but the thought of maintaining his record kept him eating hotdogs.

That was the thing about holding a record: you had to be constantly looking over your shoulder in case there was someone sneaking up behind you trying to take it away.

The bigger his record was the more daunting it would be for others to even set out to beat it. A kid would need to start eating hotdogs in third year and keep on eating them right up until they went to secondary school to beat Lee's record now, and there couldn't be many kids out there prepared to invest the time, effort and gut-rot required to meet that sort of challenge.

Will bit into his equally predictable lunch of baked potato and cheese.

'Did I tell you I'm going ahead with my tuck shop idea?' Lee said.

'But I thought your mum and dad weren't allowing you

to run one.'

'They're not.'

'You're ignoring them?'

'Yes.'

Will considered this. 'Well, it's down to you.'

Lee nodded.

'It'll be a lot of work.'

'No pain, no gain. And talking of pains ...'

Lee explained that his one worry, as far as the hiding place for his stock was concerned, was his pain of a little sister, Rebecca. She had a tendency to wander around all over the garden, which meant she could end up anywhere – including the old greenhouse. All he needed was for her to discover the boxes and trek into the house with a few bars of chocolate. Then Lee's secret would be out. So he'd rigged up a barrier over the greenhouse door. He'd dragged a piece of disused fencing across the grass and placed it where it was unlikely Rebecca would bother to move it, not least because it was heavy, even for Lee.

'So you think your stock's safe now?'

'As safe as houses,' Lee replied, swallowing his last mouthful of hotdog.

Chapter
Eleven

This was it. This was where Lee joined the road to becoming a millionaire. This was where his dream of giant swimming pools and as many toys and games as he could ever play with started to come true.

Because this was Day One.

Day One started like any other day, though. It wasn't one for feigning sickness in order to get off school, so Lee slid out of bed and put on his school clothes. He felt the usual nausea at the brown colour scheme he was forced to wear. Who'd chosen it? Someone colour-blind? A ninety-eight-year-old ex-army major who wanted pupils to wear something that would remind him of all the muck he'd made his troops shovel in the trenches during the First World War?

Next he went downstairs, where his mum was dashing about the kitchen.

'Quick, Lee. Come on. Eat your breakfast and then you'll need to get going. I'm going to be late.'

Lee's mum was always running late. She hated getting out of bed and always left it to the last minute, so every morning she flapped about in a panic, trying to get

Rebecca to dress herself but eventually doing it for her because it was quicker that way. Lee reckoned that his mum ought to take Rebecca out in her pyjamas one morning. Then she'd learn to get more of a move on.

Lee was happy to hurry today. He emptied his bowl of cereal in a minute flat, stuck his lunch money in his pocket, remembered to clean his teeth without having to be told (for once) and left his mum to concentrate on sorting out Rebecca, who had accidentally dropped most of her cereal on the kitchen floor.

It was a sunny morning and Lee felt good as he took his first steps towards fame and fortune.

He reached the corner of the road and, after checking that no-one was looking, cut up the track that ran behind the houses. A few seconds later he carefully swung open the decrepit wooden gate at the end of the garden. It didn't even creak.

Next he shifted the barrier in front of the greenhouse door just enough to allow him to slide though the gap. Once inside, he took his old schoolbag out of his new one and filled both with a selection of crisps, chocolate and chews from the boxes he'd hidden under the shelving.

There was quite a weight in the bars of chocolate, but they took up less room than the crisps and would make him more money. So he decided on a compromise and filled the bottom of the two schoolbags with confectionery before placing bags of crisps on top where their contents were less likely to get pulverised.

Duly packed, Lee closed up the greenhouse, exited the back gate and continued on his way to school, an extra spring in his step as he looked forward to profitably offloading the weight on his back.

Now his main task was to make his fellow pupils aware of his service. He'd considered wearing a sandwich board (one of those in which the person is the filling) but thought it would look stupid, and in any case he wasn't sure how the teachers would react. That was something he'd have to watch. Some teachers were always trying to stop you doing things and Lee wasn't sure how they would take to him running a multi-million pound business on the school premises. They might blackmail him into handing over a share of the profits. Worse still, they might want a say in what he sold, forcing him to sell healthy food like fruit. That would be disastrous!

So, instead of a sandwich board or leaflets, or anything else that could draw the attention of staff, he'd decided that the simplest strategy was to speak to people in person.

And his first opportunity came even before he set foot inside the school gates.

It couldn't have been a better one, because Idle Ian, the school's biggest couch potato, was known to all at school as a boy who liked a sweet or thirty-four. It was also said that his parents gave him loads of pocket money.

Perfect.

Lee didn't really know Idle Ian, but decided that shouldn't stop him introducing his new mobile tuck shop service.

'Ian,' he began.

'What?'

'I've got something that might interest you.'

'Oh yeah? Who are you?'

'I'm Lee, and from today I'm starting a mobile tuck shop. I'll be selling things cheaper than you can get them in the shops, plus you won't have to walk there to get them.'

'Oh right. What kind of things do you have?' Ian asked.

Lee realised he'd sparked Ian's interest, so he slung one of the schoolbags from his back, rested it on the ground and opened it.

'These kinds of things,' he said, making sure Idle Ian got a good eyeful of the crisps and chocolate.

'Wow! That lot would keep me going for a whole ...' Idle Ian searched for the right word.

'Morning interval?' Lee was tempted to say but didn't. Idle Ian was a potential customer. According to his own business rules, he had to be nice to him.

'... A whole month,' Idle Ian finally decided.

Lee thought that was decidedly optimistic but kept his trap shut.

'How much are they all?' Idle Ian asked.

'You want to buy them all?' Lee checked, unable to believe his ears. He knew Idle Ian ate a lot, but he hadn't realised it was that much.

'No, no. I just want to know how much each item is.'

'Aw.' Lee took out the price list he'd written down on a page ripped from one of his jotters and showed it to his customer.

Idle Ian muttered to himself as he read through it. 'Hmm ... right ... okay ... yeah, not bad ... Ah yes, and I love those ....'

Having checked out the prices, Idle Ian stuck his hand in his pocket and produced such a mountain of gold, silver and copper coinage that a whole army of beggars could have lived off it for several months. Indeed, it was a wonder his pockets hadn't burst. Maybe his mum had reinforced them.

'I'll take three bags of crisps and one of those chocolate

bars. Oh, and one of those, too,' said Idle Ian.

His first sale! Already! To someone he barely knew! And he hadn't even reached the school gates! Exclamation marks were bursting to get out of Lee but he kept his calm.

He needed to. As he was digging into his bag and taking out the crisps and chocolate bar, Idle Ian decided he'd better have some more nosh, presumably in case he was starving to death by lunchtime.

'You'd better give me one of those as well,' Idle Ian continued. 'And is that a ... oh, yes! Brilliant, they're the best ...'

'Eh, okay, so that's three lots of 26p, a 31p, a ...'

Lee began to panic. He hadn't expected one person to buy so much from him. Adding up the cost of everything was going to be complicated.

'Eh, that's, well twenty-six add twenty-six, that's, eh ... fifty-two. Add another twenty-six is, eh, is ...'

As had been the case so many times before in Lee's life, it was Will who came to the rescue.

'Hi, Lee.'

'Oh, hi.'

'So come on, how much?' Idle Ian asked, becoming impatient.

'Eh, what was I at again? Twenty-six add twenty-six is ...'

'Here,' Will said, 'borrow my calculator.'

Saved! A rainstorm had started just as he'd been about to be burned at the stake; the tide had turned just as he'd been about to drown; a cure had been found just as he'd been about to die of a terrible disease; a giant eagle had plucked him from the air just as he'd fallen off a cliff; a dragon had come along and lit a fire just as he'd been about to freeze to death from cold ...

'Come on. How much?'

'What? Oh yeah, right.' Lee realised he'd been getting somewhat carried away with the 'being saved' thing and started punching the buttons on Will's calculator. 'That's two pound sixty-eight altogether,' he said a few seconds later.

Ian wandered off after paying, already unwrapping his second breakfast.

'How about that!' Lee exclaimed to Will.

'Well done. You couldn't have picked anyone better. He'll probably buy about as much as you can carry to school each day!'

Will was right. Lee had struck gold at the first attempt. All he needed was a few more customers like Idle Ian and he'd be laughing all the way to the bank. (Of course he'd stop laughing once he got there so that the clerks didn't look at him as if he were mad. He'd maybe laugh all the way home again though.)

Chapter
Twelve

Monday mornings started with Religious Education, and that meant putting up with Miss P. That wasn't her real name – no-one has a one-letter surname – but since her real name was Mrs Pitsarovanovitchsky (her family was originally from the Ukraine, just west of Russia) and no-one could say that very well (let alone spell it), she allowed her pupils to call her Miss P. Then one of the pupils had heard another teacher call Miss P by her first name – Anita. Now pupils delighted in sticking their hands up and saying, 'Excuse me, Miss Anita P.'

Lee liked Religious Education, and not just because he could laugh at the teacher's name. He enjoyed learning about what other people believed, even though it made him wonder whether anyone was right. His dad also wondered about that, usually out loud in one of his regular rants. Oh yes, it wasn't just the royal family he went on about, he ranted about plenty of other things as well – the government, the state of the roads, the weather, the rubbish programmes on TV ... Nothing was immune from his ranting, and the older he grew the more he ranted.

But today Lee's mind wasn't on Religious Education or, indeed, education of any sort. Instead, he was looking ahead to the morning interval when he would get out amongst the crowds and find some new customers. On the back of his jotter he'd already worked out that he'd made a 68p profit on what he'd sold to Idle Ian.

Okay, so you couldn't exactly buy a house with that, but it was a start.

So when the bell rang Lee was, most unusually, first out of the door, charging along the corridor (against school rules) to reach the exit to the playground.

'Get your tuck over here!' he shouted once there, only to find himself completely ignored by his fellow pupils who were streaming past him. He called again. 'Cheap crisps and sweets! Does anyone want any?'

'What have you got?' asked a familiar voice.

It was Creepy Craig, the last person Lee wanted to see, but he opened up one of his two school bags anyway and let Craig peer in. A customer was a customer, after all.

'How much?' Craig asked, taking Lee by surprise. He'd been expecting a snide remark, not genuine interest in what he was selling. So Lee went through the prices, just as he had with Idle Ian.

'Okay, I'll take one of those,' Craig said, pointing.

'That's 32p, please,' Lee said, feeling like a proper shopkeeper.

While Creepy Craig counted out his money, one of his friends joined him. (Creeps hang about together, presumably because no-one else wants to hang out with them.)

'Hey, how's it hanging?' Number Two Creep said in what he seemed to think was a cool rapper voice, but which actually made him sound like an idiot.

'Wicked,' Creepy Craig replied. 'This dude's got some good gear.'

Did these guys always speak to each other like this or had someone put something dodgy in their cereal?

The correct answer to that question was: who cared as long as they were handing over their money? which Number Two Creep duly did in return for a bag of crisps.

'Is this a one off?' Creepy Craig asked.

'No, I'll be doing it every day,' Lee told him.

'Good.'

As Creepy Craig and his fellow dude turned to go, Lee was just beginning to think that maybe he'd misjudged them, that maybe they weren't such creeps after all. But then Craig spoiled it by turning back and saying, 'At this rate you'll soon be making enough to afford to buy girls' comics *every* week.'

'It was for ...'

'Yeah, yeah, I know. It was for your "sister".'

And with that Creepy Craig and his cretinous cohort set off for another part of the playground.

It seemed no time at all before the bell rang and Lee had to shut up shop (or shut up schoolbag) and join the other pupils heading back to their classrooms. The fifteen minutes of the morning interval had allowed him to serve exactly four customers, the last a girl in his class. It was hardly Tesco. And although he could feel the weight of his earnings in his pockets, his trousers weren't exactly hanging around his ankles from the strain. There was no need to buy braces or a stronger belt just yet.

Still, he'd made a start, and when it came to lunchtime he decided that just for once he wouldn't sprint to the canteen to be first to demolish a hotdog. He recognised that his best chance to sell to people at lunchtime was before they reached the canteen. Sane kids spent all the money they had on their lunch because if they took it home their parents would only take it back off them. Unless Lee got to them before they paid for their lunches, his fellow pupils would have nothing to spend at *Lee's Mobile Tuck Shop*, and that would be a disaster. So Lee positioned himself outside the doors of the canteen and tried to persuade all those who entered to stop and look at what he had to offer inside the two schoolbags. The problem was that all the pupils were starving and desperate to get into the queue as quickly as possible, so they weren't keen on stopping to speak or look. Lee was almost trampled in the rush.

Lee decided to follow the 'if you can't beat them, join them' saying, and eventually sat down next to Will, who was, as ever, munching away at a baked potato.

'Don't you ever get fed up eating the same thing every lunchtime?' Lee asked.

Will was astounded. 'Me? Look who's talking! What about you and your hotdogs?'

It was a fair point. Even Lee had to admit that he probably kept at least one hotdog-making factory in business throughout the year, thus protecting the livelihoods of many workers and ensuring they had enough income to put food on the tables of their families. (Lee wondered if those workers put the same food on their tables as they made for his lunches, or did they get sick of seeing it all day every day?)

Will rose from his seat. 'Are you coming out to the playground? It's dry ...'

'Yes.' Lee indicated his schoolbag. 'But I need to try and sell some more of this stuff first before I can play.'

And it turned out that not everyone had spent all their money on school dinners, so Lee had some success in the playground after lunch. He observed that kids' appetites suddenly returned at the very sight of confectionery.

However, Lee's initial success prompted him to consider two problems he knew he would encounter in the future. The first was where to put his vast wealth. He couldn't put it under his pillow. Even though he was forced to make his own bed, his mum still changed his pyjamas and would find it. He could put it under his mattress, as some old people apparently still did, but what if his mum and dad decided to turn that over or replace it? No, the only truly safe place would be a bank. But could kids his age open a bank account, especially without their parents finding out? There wasn't much he could do about it during the afternoon at school, but he needed to find out soon. Jars in the greenhouse weren't a long-term solution. What if someone broke in and stole them?

And then there was the second problem (or 'issue' as his dad would call it – even 'opportunity' if he was really getting into management speak that day). How could he spend his money without making his new-found wealth too obvious? If new bikes and games were delivered to the door it might raise a few suspicions; likewise if a chauffeur-driven car pulled up outside to take him the few hundred metres to school.

But what was the point of having lots of money if you couldn't spend it?

In Lee's opinion there was no point whatsoever. Absolutely none. It would be a waste. Money was for buying things, not for hoarding. You couldn't play with bank statements, no matter how big the balance. (Not unless you were desperate for drawing paper and used the backs of them.)

It was only during project work later that day that Lee realised the reality of his monetary situation, recalling what Uncle Raymond had said during their discussion back on the farm. 'If you spend all the money you make from selling the first load, you won't be able to buy any more to sell, so you'll need to reinvest it.'

And so Lee decided to postpone a visit to the bank for the moment. He'd deposit his millions the following month instead.

Chapter
Thirteen

Business grew steadily over the next week. Those who'd already bought from him were happy to do so again, and when their friends saw them buying, they too took advantage of Lee's service. At the beginning of the week Lee was selling just a handful of items; by the end he was selling more than half of what he could fit into his two schoolbags. Soon the time would come when he'd be unable to carry enough to school in the mornings to satisfy his customers throughout the day. Perhaps he'd need to consider nipping home at lunchtime to restock. However, that wouldn't be easy; pupils weren't supposed to leave the school grounds at any time during the day.

'It's like Colditz, that castle where the Germans used to lock up their enemies in World War II,' Lee remarked to Will. 'We're prisoners here.'

'In that case ...'

'What? In that case what?' Will usually came up with good ideas so Lee was keen to hear what he had to say.

'Well, if you can't leave the school once you're here, maybe you could find somewhere to store stuff in school.'

'I'm not sure about that ...'

'I don't mean all of it. Just what you need for that day. Say you could find a cupboard you could stash it in first thing in the morning. Then you could stock up from there whenever you needed to. And if you only left it there during the day ...'

'... then the janitor and the cleaners shouldn't find it,' Lee finished for him.

'Exactly.'

'Will,' Lee said, putting a hand on his friend's shoulder, 'you're a genius.'

So, with the exception of deciding which cupboard to use as his stash, that was that problem/issue/opportunity resolved.

Lee looked up and grinned. However, his smile soon faded. It was there again, that face at the window. That was twice now, and on neither occasion had it lingered long enough for him to recognise it.

Was he imagining things? Was his brain playing tricks, making him think others were out to get him when they weren't?

No, he was absolutely convinced that he was being spied on. Why else did the person disappear as soon as he turned his head towards them?

It was on his way home that he made a dreadful discovery.

It was a discovery Lee wouldn't have made if he hadn't happened to look over his shoulder just after he was past his adversary's shop.

Perhaps it was the memory of Panface appearing at his shoulder in that same shop that led Lee to look back. Perhaps it was a feeling of guilt at taking away so much of Panface's trade. Or perhaps it was the fact that his mum had once said that Panface looked and acted like the sort of man who might run a Shopkeepers' Mafia. Whatever it was, it was just as well that he did look back.

Panface stepped into the doorway of his shop and stood there, eyes following Lee's every step. Lee tried to walk on without looking back again, but he couldn't. And when he turned once more, to his horror he saw Jani Tor, his school's caretaker, approaching Panface. Not only that, but as she did so she pointed at Lee.

Lee was already walking quickly, but now increased his speed even more in a bid to reach the relative safety of his home before the shopkeeper and caretaker got their act together and set off after him.

As his legs sped under him Lee tried to figure out what

had gone wrong. How had Jani found out what he was doing? And why was she telling Panface?

The answer was obvious: Jani was Panface's spy.

That had to be it. Panface had become so concerned about the decline in sales at his shop that he'd started paying Jani to find out what was going on. She was his perfect spy, able to roam freely around the school, able to speak to kids and check the contents of rubbish bins ... whatever it took.

And now she was reporting back just as Lee, her chief suspect, was passing.

What should he do? If the two of them set off after him they would be at the house in minutes. They might not find his stock, but they'd tell his mum, who would be home by now, and then he'd be in big trouble. Seriously big trouble. The sort of big trouble that's the trouble equivalent of the Empire State Building, or even the Taipei 101 Tower in Taiwan, which is another one third taller than the Empire State Building, topping out at 509 metres. Imagine that. More than half a kilometre into the sky, with 101 storeys and an 800-metric-ton ball-shaped damper near the top to help counter swaying during earthquakes and typhoons. Anyway, the point is, this was really big trouble for Lee, as you'll probably have gathered by now.

So what could he do about it?

Not a lot.

If he told his mum he'd be in twice as much trouble for going behind her back and starting his mobile tuck shop, as well as for taking away much of Panface's business. If he didn't tell her then he'd still have to face Panface and Jani Tor when they arrived at the door.

Lee called hello to his mum as he entered the house, then climbed the stairs two at a time as he headed for the toilet, where he locked himself in. When the knock on the door came he would climb out of the window onto the kitchen roof and then jump into the garden to escape the clutches of the shop owner and caretaker. What he would do after that he had no idea. Perhaps he'd have a few seconds to grab some stock from the greenhouse as he made his escape, in which case he could flee to Scotland and set up his business there. No-one would go looking for him there; the weather was too bad.

Lee had a quick pee in case he had to run for a long time without being able to go to the toilet. As he washed his hands he threw water on his hair and tried to give himself a new hairstyle so that he would be less recognisable when escaping and when people were out looking for him, comparing him to the pictures the police would issue across the country. Under his photo (hopefully not the one of him sitting naked in the bath – the one his mum seemed to delight in showing everyone) it would say:

WANTED

LEE WATERS

FOR STEALING PANFACE'S CUSTOMERS AND ILLEGALLY SELLING TUCK AT SCHOOL (AND NOT EVEN TELLING HIS PARENTS HE WAS DOING IT)

Lee checked his watch. He'd been home for fifteen minutes.

'Lee, are you okay?' he heard him mum call up. 'Are you constipated? Do you want something to help unblock you?'

'No, I'm fine. I'm just reading a book,' Lee called back.

That seemed to satisfy his mum, who was always pleased when Lee settled down to some reading. But it wouldn't satisfy Panface and Jani Tor when they came knocking. They wouldn't care if he'd read every book ever written, they'd still want to tear him limb from limb.

So where were they?

Another ten minutes went by and Lee heard footsteps climbing the stairs.

'Come on, Lee. I'm bursting,' his mum called through the door. 'You can read in your bedroom if you want.'

It seemed that he didn't have any choice. He flushed the toilet again to make it seem as if he'd only just finished.

'Don't forget to bring your book out.'

'I haven't ... oh no, I've flushed it down the toilet!'

'What?!'

'I didn't put the seat cover down and then I left the book on the edge of the toilet bowl and it must have fallen in while I was washing my hands.'

Lee opened the bathroom door.

'Oh for goodness sake, Lee! Try to be more careful. I wouldn't be surprised if you've blocked the toilet up.'

'Eh, it was only a small, thin book.'

'Which one was it?'

'It was ... *How To Get Great Marks At School*.'

'Oh that's good. Where did you get that one from?'

'The library. They have loads of great books. But don't worry, I'm sure the librarian will be very understanding when I explain to her what happened, Mum. We won't have to buy them another one. Librarians are great people.'

'I hope so,' his mum said, closing the toilet door behind her and saying, 'There's less of a stink in here than I expected ....'

There was still no knock from Panface and Jani Tor. What was going on? Did they have such short memories that they'd forgotten about him already? (Unlikely. He was confusing them with the rest of his classmates.) Could it be that they didn't know where he lived and had gone up to the school to find out? Or could it be ...

Could it be that he'd got it all wrong? (Let's face it, it wouldn't have been the first time.) Could it be that Jani Tor had been pointing him out as just *one* of the suspects – that in fact every kid in the school was currently under suspicion?

Lee hardly dared to hope, but as the afternoon wore on he began to relax. They didn't know about him. He was in the clear.

There were a lot of weeds in Upa Blin Dali's garden. A lot more than Lee had bargained for. He stood and looked at the numerous flowerbeds cut into the lawn, all of which had a carpet of small, green, leaves covering them. Why couldn't Mr Dali have left the lawn alone? What had possessed him to cut chunks out of it to plant a few flowers and, at the same time, provide an ideal living space for weeds? He'd made work for himself. A lot of work. And now he'd passed that work on.

Still, at least he was getting paid for this work, Lee reminded himself. He supposed that in some respects he ought to be grateful for all the weeds. Without them, there wouldn't be a job to do.

Mr Dali had left some equipment at the rear of the house for Lee to use: a spade, a hoe and a trowel. He'd also left a short note:

Dear Lee
I know it's only Spring and so a long time until Christmas, but hoe, hoe, hoe anyway!
Regards,
Upa Blin Dali

Lee's dad had obviously been speaking to Mr Dali, and somehow during their conversation Mr Dali had become infected with Lee's dad's sense of humour. What other explanation was there for such a dreadful joke?

Lee decided to start in the front garden, near the gate, where the impact of his efforts would be immediately visible to Mr Dali when the hardworking restaurateur arrived home from work late that evening. And if Mr Dali immediately noticed a difference, then he was likely to carry on paying Lee to look after his garden.

Lee had been at pains to point out to his parents that just because he was tackling gardening work didn't mean he had suddenly developed a love of gardening itself. 'This has nothing to do with gardening,' he'd told his mum that afternoon as he'd set off for Mr Dali's. 'It's about money.'

Even such a blunt statement had not entirely extin - guished Lee's mum's hopes. 'Well, perhaps being out there amongst all those wonderful flowers will give you a new interest in nature. You never know.'

Lee very much doubted it. Plants were for old people, so even if he did unexpectedly find himself learning the names of some of them, he certainly wouldn't be admitting it to anyone.

Mrs Dali was away, too. She worked just as hard as Mr

Dali. Five afternoons a week she helped out in an old people's home (where they presumably loved talking about plants), and then six days a week she joined Mr Dali at the restaurant in the evening. It was no wonder that between them they had little time or energy left for gardening.

With hoe in hand, Lee set about tidying up the front garden. It had rained at lunchtime, softening the earth and making it easy to move. The hoe skimmed effortlessly through the top few centimetres, dislodging everything in its path that wasn't already a good height. Lee was surprised at just how many weeds had grown between the flowers, but that was weeds for you; they jumped at any piece of empty ground that came their way.

After finishing the first flowerbed Lee took a rest and surveyed his efforts. Yes, it looked a whole lot better. Only flowers remained in the earth. With everything else removed from around them they would be able to breathe more easily and soak up a larger share of any rain that fell. There wouldn't be any greedy weeds trying to hog the light and water for themselves. Lee was proud of what he'd achieved.

Perhaps Mr and Mrs Dali would even think about planting a few more flowers now that Lee had performed the hard work of clearing the ground for them. The first flowerbed looked rather empty now he'd finished hoeing it.

With this thought in mind (along with a picture of a smiling, happy Mr and Mrs Dali returning home from work), Lee set about clearing the second flowerbed as ruthlessly as the first. Anything that didn't have a flower on it went.

Thrusting the hoe back and forth was hard work and it wasn't long before the muscles in Lee's arm began to ache. So he took a breather, perching himself on Mr and Mrs Dali's doorstep.

As he sat there he peered over the hedge and saw his mum climbing the hill towards him.

'Hiya,' she said as she reached the gate. She had a glass of juice in her hand.

'How's Mummy's Little Worker doing, eh?'

'He's thirsty.'

'I thought he might be.' She handed him the glass and took a seat next to him. 'So how are you getting on so far?'

Lee drank most of the juice in a oner, then, recovering his breath, said, 'Pretty good. I've finished those two beds already.' He pointed to where the earth had been skimmed and turned.

'Have you shifted many weeds?'

'Loads.'

'You must have, because I can't see a single one!'

'I raked them off and dumped them over there.' With an outstretched finger Lee indicated the pile he'd created at the edge of the grass. 'I'll stick everything on Mr Dali's compost heap when I'm finished.'

'Gosh, that's quite a stack.'

Lee grinned.

'Were there some very big weeds in there?'

'Monster-sized,' Lee said. 'You should have seen the roots on some of them. I had to dig down to get them out.'

Lee's mum stood up and wandered over to the pile of weeds. She bent down, picked up one of the larger ones and held it before her eyes, examining it. Then she put it back down and picked up another couple of samples.

'Those weeds were making the garden look really untidy,' Lee told his mum. 'Mr Dali's going to be so chuffed when he sees what I've done, don't you think?'

Lee's mum turned around on her haunches until she was facing him. 'Lee, these weeds you've dug up ...'

'Yes ...'

'They're not weeds. They're flowers!' She showed him the first 'weed' she'd lifted from the pile. 'These ones are poppies. And these,' – she held aloft a second 'weed' – 'these are pansies.'

Lee felt sick. 'But how can they be flowers if they haven't got any flowers on them?'

'Different plants produce flowers at different times of the year, Lee. Some in Spring, some in Summer and so on. Just because a plant doesn't have petals doesn't mean it's a weed!'

Lee slapped the whole of the palm of one hand across his forehead. 'Aw,' he said despondently.

'I don't know what Mr Dali's going to want to do to you when he realises what you've done,' his mum said.

Lee had a few ideas as to what Mr and Mrs Dali might contemplate. Chief among them was force-feeding Lee the hottest curry from their restaurant, with red chillies as a compulsory accompaniment.

'What can I do? Can I stick them all back in the ground?'

Lee's mum shook her head. 'There's no point. You've cut the foliage off from the roots. If you stick them in the ground they'll just die.'

Lee groaned. 'I can't believe this. My first day working for Mr Dali and I've dug up half his garden! It's a disaster!'

His mum put an arm around his shoulder. (Lee was pleased to see that it was her own arm, and not just someone's she'd found lying about.) He could feel tears forming. A disaster was unfolding and he was its unfor -

tunate victim.

'I'm sure there's something we can do,' his mum told him.

'Do we have any of the same flowers in our garden? The same ones I've dug up here?'

'Why?'

'Well we could plant our ones in Mr Dali's garden. He'd never notice.'

His mum didn't relish the prospect of losing all the flowers in her garden. 'I don't think that's necessary,' she said. 'It was just a mistake.'

'Well I've got to do something, Mum! I can't leave it as it is. Mr Dali will sack me, and this is the first day I've been on the job!'

Lee no longer had the will to hold on to the hoe he'd been clasping in his hand. He let it fall to the ground, where it landed with a clatter. The noise acted like the bell of his alarm clock first thing in the morning: it roused him and brought him to his senses.

'The garden centre, then,' he said. 'Could we replace them with new ones from the garden centre?'

'We could. But plants cost money, you know.'

'How much?'

'To replace that lot?' Lee's mum nodded at the pile of greenery that had been torn out before it had even had a chance to reach its prime. 'A good few quid.'

'I could pay you back, though.'

'What with?'

'With the money Mr Dali's going to give me for doing the garden.'

'Do you honestly think he'll still pay you after this ...?'

'He will if he thinks I've done a good job.'

'But Lee, you've ...'

'I know, Mum, I know. But if we go to the garden centre, buy some replacement plants and stick them in the ground before Mr and Mrs Dali get home ... then they won't be able to tell the difference.'

'But they'll be different plants. We'll never be able to match them all exactly.'

Lee thought about this for a second, then said, 'That won't matter. I only cut down the ones that didn't have any flowers on, so as long as the ones we get are just green, he won't be able to tell the difference. Plus, if he notices there are some he didn't have before ... well, I'll say it's because of the great job I've done.'

'I don't quite follow you there ...'

Lee was on a roll. 'I'll say that they were there all the time, except that he couldn't notice them because the weeds were blocking them out. That way he'll think I've done a fantastic job – that everything in his garden is so much healthier than before and growing so well. And it'll convince him to keep me on as his gardener!'

'Well, maybe ...'

'And if Mr Dali keeps me on, I'll be able to pay you back whatever it costs to buy the replacement plants for his garden.'

Lee's mum considered this. 'It's not being entirely honest though, is it?'

'But if it makes Mr Dali happy and the only cost is to me, what's wrong with it?'

'You'd definitely pay me back?' Lee's mum checked.

'Definitely, Mum. Hand on heart and hope to die.'

'Hmm. Well, okay, seeing as you're trying to do the right thing and since you've already put some work in with the best of intentions.'

'Thanks, Mum. Can we go straight to the garden centre? Like right now?'

'We'll need to if you're going to get everything planted before Mr Dali gets back.'

Fortunately Lee and his mum managed to pick up a few bargains at the garden centre, but it was still expensive considering the hourly rate Lee had agreed with Mr Dali. As he dug holes and popped the new plants in, he worked out that the purchases had cost him a full three weeks' pay.

The planting was a slog. It was nine-thirty and almost dark before Lee finally finished. So he was exhausted when he traipsed into the kitchen and sat down at the table.

'Done?' Lee's mum asked.

Lee summoned enough strength to nod his head, before laying it on his arms on the table, eyelids heavy.

'Well, I'm proud of you for sorting it all out,' his mum said. 'You could have just thrown up your hands and left it all for Mr Dali to contend with, but you didn't, you took the initiative and rectified your mistakes, which is one of the attitudes that marks out a good businessman. So good on you.'

'Thanks.' He raised his head again. 'Mum, I'm going to bed,' he said. 'I'm knackered.' And with that he climbed the stairs and slid under his covers, still fully clothed. Two minutes later he was asleep.

' Dogs. Don't you just love them?' said Al Satian, the man who lived across the street from Lee.

'Not really,' would have been the honest answer, but Lee didn't say that. It would be bad for business. Instead he said, 'Yes, they're great, aren't they?'

'Man's best friend. No doubt about it.'

Al's dog, Rogan, certainly seemed to want to be friends with Lee, if the way his paws were resting against Lee's chest was anything to go by.

'Down, Rogan!' Al instructed. Reluctantly, Rogan returned his paws to the ground, trotted around Al twice, then sat on Lee's feet.

'Oh, well, that's you two mates for life,' Al joked. 'Once he sits on your feet there's no going back.'

And that's me got flat feet for life, Lee thought. Rogan was heavy. Lee shuffled back, trying to free his feet from under Rogan's rear end, but Rogan matched him move for move.

'Now, are you sure you'll be okay if you take him out?' Al checked. 'You've dealt with dogs before, I take it?'

'Oh yes, lots of times. I love them. They're great fun.'

This wasn't entirely a lie, more a bending of the truth, because Lee certainly had dealt with dogs lots of times before. Usually it had been when he and Will had been playing football in the park, and usually he'd dealt with those dogs by chasing them away before they could burst the ball with their sharp teeth...Or by running from them if they showed those sharp teeth.

'Then you shouldn't have any problems. Just make sure he knows you're the boss or he'll try to get his own way.'

Lee bent down, rubbed Rogan under the chin and said, 'We're going to get on just fine, aren't we?' Rogan whined pitifully in reply.

'That means "yes",' Al said.

'If that's "yes" then what does "no" sound like?'

'He doesn't really say "no", he just runs off and hides under the kitchen table.'

'Aw.'

'Don't you?' Al said to Rogan as if speaking to a two-year-old child. He stuck his face up against Rogan's snout, a brave move given how close it took him to Rogan's slobber machine.

'Where are you thinking of taking him?' Al asked Lee.

'Oh, just around the block a few times to begin with. I might take him to the park once we get to know each other better. It'll give us both a change of scenery.'

'Good idea. Now, you'll be needing his lead.' Al stepped into his house and returned a moment later with Rogan's lead. As soon as Rogan saw it he leapt from Lee's foot and headed to the furthest corner of the garden.

'He thinks he's going somewhere bad,' Al explained. 'We usually only put the lead on him if we're taking him to the vet or the kennels.'

Lee tried some encouragement. 'Walkies, Rogan!' he called. 'Come on! Walkies!'

Rogan pretended to have found something very in - teresting under the hedge, something that required his total and undivided attention. In other words, he com- pletely ignored Lee.

'I'm afraid that 'walkies' isn't a word he hears very much these days,' Al admitted. 'He's probably forgotten what it means. However, I'm sure he'll soon remember after he's been out a few times with you.'

Al handed Lee the lead and Lee hid it behind his back as he approached Rogan.

Rogan was a stupid dog. But he wasn't that stupid. He knew exactly where the lead was, so he waited until Lee was less than a metre away before bounding off to the opposite end of the garden.

Al laughed. Lee smiled weakly. An unruly dog wasn't what he needed. It was bad enough having an unruly sister.

After a ten-minute chase Al was eventually able to attach the lead to Rogan's collar. Al showed Lee the best way to hold the lead – putting it over his wrist and then into his hand – and told him of things to watch out for – cats, birds, squirrels, children, trees, bicycles, cars, postmen and other dogs, to name but a few – then Lee dragged Rogan to the gate.

'Have fun,' Al called.

'Will do.'

Once they were beyond the gate it didn't take Rogan long to figure out that Lee wasn't taking him anywhere bad, so he perked up and focused his attention on the extremely important task of sniffing anything and everything they passed. One moment Lee would be walking along at a brisk pace, the next his arm would be wrenched from its socket as Rogan slammed on the brakes without warning, having picked up a trail. Every time he did so he cocked a leg and left his scent for the rest of the dog world to smell when it passed. It was dog graffiti. **ROGAN WOZ HERE**. Although the colour wasn't strong, one could be pretty certain the stench was.

After realising that he was actually in for a good time,

Rogan set a blistering pace. At least he attempted to. Lee couldn't keep up unless he ran, and he had no intention of running the whole way. Walkies were so-called for a reason, so he tugged on the lead to give Rogan the message to slow down. As Al had said, it was important that Rogan knew who was boss.

But if Lee was the boss, Rogan was a rotten employee. If he'd been human, Lee would have sacked him. He kept on tugging at the lead, dragging Lee along, as if the very next gatepost – and then the next and the next – would reveal the key to eternal dog happiness provided he reached it in time.

Eventually Lee decided he'd had enough. He stopped, forcing Rogan to stand still against his will. 'Sit!' Lee instructed. Rogan whined. 'Sit!' Lee repeated, determined to instil some discipline in the dog. Rogan whined some more, then sat on Lee's foot, just as he had earlier.

'No, no, not there!' Lee prised his foot out from under the dog's backside. 'Now, if you and I are going to get along – and frankly we don't have much choice because you want your walks and I want my wages – then you're going to have to take things more calmly, okay?'

It did get better, though. After five minutes Rogan calmed down and settled into a gentle bouncing stride, occasionally even letting his lead fall slack. Lee supposed that Rogan's behaviour was understandable. He was hardly ever taken out for a walk like this, so he wanted to make the most of it.

Lee had decided on a circular walk so they would never be too far from the Satian family's home. However, three-quarters of the way round, Rogan stopped. Stopped and would not budge.

There didn't appear to be any reason for him stopping. Lee looked around in case the dumb mutt had spotted something that required so much of his attention that he couldn't move at the same time, but there was nothing. He also listened carefully in case there was a noise that he hadn't picked up. He knew that dogs could hear much higher frequencies than humans, so maybe that was it. Having both looked and listened, Lee checked Rogan's face for a tell-tale look of concentration, but found none. Instead he saw stubbornness.

'Now don't you start that with me,' Lee ordered. But Rogan stood his ground defiantly, refusing to be intim-idated. 'Come on!' Lee tried again. Still no movement. 'Is it that you're having such a great time that you don't want to go back?' Lee asked.

Rogan didn't answer, but his expression changed to what

Lee was sure was one of contentment. Yes, that was it, he'd stopped because he was overcome with joy at being allowed to walk outside for more than two minutes. He was relishing the chance to be out in the open air, taking in new sights, sounds and smells. He was at one with nature. He could see himself as a free dog again, running wild with the pack and chasing rabbits and ...

And pooing wherever he wanted, just as he was now.

'Oh man!' Lee cried. 'You can't do that there, in the middle of the pavement! At least go into the gutter!'

Rogan appeared not to have learned the subtle, but rather important, difference between pavements and gutters.

Lee knew that dog owners had to scoop up anything their dog did in the street. They weren't allowed to leave poos to rot. Young children might pick them up and take them home to use as toys, or they might mistake them for a new style of chocolatey treat and attempt to eat them. So Lee had been sent out with just a couple of bags, but with Al assuring him that it was very unlikely that Rogan would do anything outside of the garden.

Oh really? In that case, what was the pile of steaming, stinky, sludgy poo that had just landed in the middle of the pavement, courtesy of Rogan's bowels?

Rogan actually looked quite pleased with himself. He raised his head and eyes as if to say, 'Look at the size of that one, Lee!'

Lee *was* looking at the size of it. What did Rogan eat? And for how long had he been saving all that up?

What could Lee do? There were only two options: pick it up, or walk away quickly and hope that flies were quick eaters.

But at that precise time of day it seemed that the entire population of Lee's neighbourhood had moved outside. There was barely a garden without someone in it. And to top it all, a lady wearing the uniform of one of the local superstores was walking towards him.

'Ah, what a lovely dog,' she cooed as if Rogan was a six-month-old child. 'And look what you've done! You're very healthy, aren't you?' Having spoken to Rogan, she turned to Lee. 'Have you got a bag with you?'

'Eh...'

'Ugh. It always feels so hot and slimy when you pick it up with your hands like that, even if you know you've got a bag over them.'

This was not the sort of encouragement Lee needed.

The woman was showing no sign of carrying on along her way to work. She seemed to be waiting for Lee to get out the bag and lift the poo, as if relishing the prospect of him feeling it squidge through his fingers.

He had no choice. He stuck his hand in his pocket, pulled out the green bag, prised it apart and bent down.

Which was when the stench rose up.

'Man alive!' he cried.

'They can stink a bit,' the woman commented. Then, turning to Rogan, she said, 'Can't they?' and Rogan tried to lick her face.

Leaning as far back as possible to minimise the smell, Lee crouched and tried to slide the bag under the poo, but the horrible brown muck was too heavy.

'You've just got to grab hold of it,' the woman said. 'Get stuck in there. Imagine it's a big blob of ice cream.'

Lee had never seen or smelled anything less like ice-cream than what he was about to pick up.

'Chocolate flavour, of course,' the woman added.

If there was a world record for picking up poos then Lee broke it there and then. No sooner was it off the ground in his reluctant bag-covered hand than he had turned the plastic inside out and tied the ends. He held it as far from his body as possible.

'Just as well it's bin day, eh?' the woman said, nodding at a green rubbish bin at the end of the next drive. 'At least you won't have to carry it home in your pocket.'

Lee ran to the bin, flipped the lid and dropped the bag inside. In the confined space the poo stank even more.

'Cheerio,' the woman called as she continued on her way to work, probably to have a laugh during her tea-break by telling all her colleagues how she'd watched a boy pick up a huge poo with only a bag over his hands.

Throughout their walk Lee had been keeping a close eye on Rogan's mouth in case of a slobber attack. And now that he was moving again, evidence of a giant one was beginning to spill over Rogan's gums. All it needed was a shake of his head. Lee allowed Rogan to walk a little further in front of him, conscious that slobber attacks were usually sideways manoeuvres.

When Lee had almost reached home again he met Will heading down the road.

'Good timing,' Lee said. 'I take it you were coming to get me.'

'Eh, actually, I was heading down to Asad's.'

'The supermarket?'

'No, Asad, not Asda. He's the new kid in my class.'

'Oh. Right. You weren't coming for me then.'

'Not this time, I thought you'd be too busy. Sorting out your business or ... or walking Rogan.'

'Well, yeah, kind of. But ...'

'And haven't you got to do Mr Dali's garden tonight?'

'For a couple of hours, yes, but ...'

'And that Maths homework?'

'There is that ...'

'Well, that's why I'm not heading to yours. I've done my homework, and Asad was doing his as soon as he got home. But we're going to the park if you've got time to come along later.'

'Yeah, I will.'

'Okay,' Will said, walking on. 'Maybe see you there then.'

Soon they were drawing close to the Satian's house and Lee wondered what Rogan's reaction would be to nearing home again. The last thing Lee needed was Rogan refusing to go in the front gate.

Lee needn't have worried. As soon as Rogan realised that home was in sight, he was desperate to get back and dragged Lee along again, as he had at the start of their walk. Much as he'd obviously enjoyed being out and about, you could get too much of a good thing. Plus, in the twenty minutes that you'd been away you just never knew if another dog was going to nick your comfortable, reassuring spot under the kitchen table.

Al was in his garden. 'Hi, Lee. How did you get on? Who took who for a walk?'

'Rogan took me for the first and last sections, but it was fine the rest of the time. I think he was just excited about being out, and he certainly enjoyed it.'

This was a paying customer Lee was talking to and Lee decided it was best to tell a customer that things had gone well – that there had been no problems whatsoever. That had been how he'd handled the fiasco with Upa Blin Dali's garden. The customer didn't need to know if he wasn't affected.

Lee released Rogan from his lead. Rogan didn't bother saying hello to his owner, instead he ran straight for the back door.

'Well, if he sleeps all evening and keeps out of our way then you'll be doing us a big favour,' Al said. 'Oh, and is it okay if I pay you at the end of each week?'

'Sure.' The very thought of pay had Lee salivating almost as much as Rogan, but fortunately slobbering rather less.

Another morning, another instance of leaving through the front door and sneaking round to the back gate to load up with stock from the greenhouse.

It was raining. Lee checked to ensure that none of the stock was getting soaked from the water dripping in through holes in the windows. It was all fine. Even if water were to drip through, everything he'd bought had its own wrapper, so he could be confident that nothing would be ruined.

Lee stuffed as much as he could into his two bags. Word was spreading and sales were improving as a result. In the first few days he had returned with his bags half full, but recently that had fallen to just a third.

Until now, Lee hadn't had to involve Will because he didn't think there was much he could do to help. And anyway, involving someone else would mean paying them, which would leave less profit for himself. However, now that business was booming, Lee realised he would soon need additional help.

Morning interval was proving to be his busiest time. It was amazing how soon after breakfast kids could feel hungry again. Also, his regulars were well aware that if they didn't get in early they would have little to choose from later in the day, which only added to the rush. An extra pair of hands – and an extra brain to calculate the costs – would be useful. Lee decided to try to make time to talk to Will about it that lunchtime.

If Will were to become more involved it might have the added advantage that they'd actually get to see each other occasionally. Lee was so busy during the intervals that he never saw Will then, and at lunchtimes it was rare for more than a couple of minutes to go by without interruption from a customer.

It wasn't much different outside of school hours. Taking Rogan for a walk every evening, washing Holly Arthanthou's car every Saturday morning and gardening at Upa Blin Dali's for a couple of hours every fortnight was taking up a large slice of Lee's life. Add to that his homework and weekly Taekwondo class and it didn't leave a lot of time for seeing his best friend.

But his toil was bringing rewards. Despite the hiccup with Mr Dali's garden, Lee's earnings were increasing steadily. He was still some way from knocking the Queen off her place in the list of the country's richest people, but at least when he did, he would be able to tell his dad that he had earned all of his vast wealth through his own hard work, unlike the monarch. He knew that would be a proud moment for his dad. It might even stop him ranting for a few weeks.

Lunchtime came around slowly. It was hard for Lee not to wish away the hours between each break because those hours were interrupting his money-making. The only long division he wanted to do these days was dividing the amount of money he made each interval by the number of minutes in it, in other words: earnings per minute. It was important to calculate this because he only had fifteen minutes for each morning interval and one hour at lunchtime. Those lengths of time would never change, so he had to ensure that he sold as much as he could during them.

He'd recently begun to wonder if he might have to sacrifice his hotdog-eating record in order to sell more at lunchtimes. If he switched to packed lunches he could eat sandwiches while serving customers. They wouldn't mind, plus that way he wouldn't suffer from the indigestion brought on by eating his hotdog too quickly in his dash to dish out the goodies and rake in the cash.

Lee used lunchtime to suggest to Will that he should take up the position of Manager that they'd previously discussed. But his best friend's response was a lot less enthusiastic than Lee had hoped for.

'I know it's great to have money,' Will said, 'but you need to have a life too. I've hardly seen you lately. You didn't make it to the park last night, did you.'

'It was too late by the time I'd finished everything. But that's the point: we'll be able to see much more of each other if we're working together.'

'Yeah, we'll certainly be together; but we'll also be working.'

Lee thought that was a bit obvious. 'Eh ... so?'

'So, we'll see each other, and if we're lucky we might even get to talk as well. For a few seconds at a time. But it's hardly ... what is it your mum's always saying ... oh, yes, "quality time". It's hardly that, is it?'

'Maybe not, but you'll be able to earn good money.'

'I realise that. But, to be honest, I'm not sure it's something I want to do any more.'

'You don't want to earn lots of money?'

Will shrugged.

Lee threw his hands up in despair (but caught them again before they fell to the ground). 'But you haven't even given it a chance!'

'I'm not sure that I want to.'

Lee was perplexed. He was also sliding along his seat, itching to get outside and conscious that this conversation was eating into precious selling time. 'I don't understand. Why not?'

'Because I don't want to become like you!'

Lee was taken aback. 'What do you mean?'

'You've changed. I know you never could keep still in a seat, but look at you now. You treat every second as if wasting it will cost you a million pounds.'

'Not a million. Well, not yet ...'

'That's what I mean! You've probably worked out exactly how much it *is* costing you. You're not relaxed any more. All you talk about these days is money.'

'I don't.'

Will didn't contradict him verbally, but raised his eyebrows in disbelief.

'Okay, so what if I do?' Lee said. 'Money's important. One day we'll both be out there in the big bad world and we'll need to earn a living.'

'I know that. But money isn't everything. We're only kids. If we don't have fun while we're growing up, when are we going to have it?'

Lee thought the answer was straightforward. 'When we're rich. I'll be able to do loads of fun things then. In fact, I'll be able to do whatever I want.'

Will shrugged. 'It's up to you.'

Lee slid along the bench. 'You're mad. This is the best opportunity you'll ever get.'

'Maybe so,' Will told him. 'But I'm still not convinced I want to take it.'

Lee grabbed his two schoolbags and headed out into the playground, baffled but already concentrating on the practicalities of business.

The weather had improved. The rain had stopped but it was still murky. Lee had learned that these were perfect conditions for selling more snacks. In dull weather his fellow pupils wanted to cheer themselves up, and what better way than with something from *Lee's Mobile Tuck Shop*. Also, dull weather meant it was quite cold, especially when the wind blew, and what better way to warm yourself up than with … something from *Lee's Mobile Tuck Shop*. Likewise, if giant puddles on the ground meant it was difficult to play football with a tennis ball, what could be better than relaxing with something from *Lee's Mobile Tuck Shop*. Etc, etc, etc.

Lee was disappointed with Will's attitude. If Will proved to be incredibly successful at something, then Lee would be delighted for him. And if whatever it was made Will a lot of money, Lee would make a point of remaining Will's best friend – in case any of that money went spare. So why wasn't Will being equally supportive? Did he resent Lee's success? Lee didn't think so. After all, although Will didn't want to work with him, he hadn't suggested they shouldn't remain friends.

In which case maybe Will was simply overawed by the speed and scale of Lee's rise to fame and fortune – that he was worried about being left in the shadows while the bright spotlights focused on Lee. That would be understandable. Will wouldn't want to be left behind. Lee was his best friend and he wouldn't want to lose him.

But another thought began to nag at Lee. What if Will was only interested in being around him *because* of the money Lee was now making? What if he was becoming a hanger-on, no longer interested in Lee as a person, keen to be around him only because he hoped to somehow benefit from Lee's success?

Money could affect people in lots of different ways.

Lee was only glad it hadn't changed his own outlook

on life.

Business was brisk that afternoon. It was a Friday, the day most kids got their pocket money and also the day most of them spent a fortune at *Lee's Mobile Tuck Shop*.

The crowd around Lee grew rapidly, pupils jostling to be served first. Lee tapped away furiously at the calculator he now carried everywhere, but still he couldn't get through everyone. The older, taller pupils used their brawn to push to the front, but not even they were able to get all of what they wanted. The huddle around Lee remained as the bell went. And then it suddenly disappeared.

Lee looked up to see why.

Jani Tor! She was approaching with long strides of her not-so-long legs.

'Lee Waters!'

Lee froze, calculator still in hand.

Jani Tor stepped right up to him.

'What are you up to? Why aren't you going back to class like everyone else, hmmm?'

It was the 'hmmm' that worried Lee. It was a hmmm that suggested she knew exactly what was going on but was making her victim spell it out nonetheless.

'Would you like me to go and get Mrs Ogilvy to speak to you?'

'No thanks.'

'Well then?'

'I was just doing some last minute homework.'

Jani Tor raised a disbelieving eyebrow.

'You know what The Og ... I mean Mrs Ogilvy is like.

I'd be dead meat if I went in before I finished my Maths, so I was just checking over the answers.' Lee held up his calculator. 'I think I've got them sorted now.'

'And I'm expected to believe you?'

'Eh ... yes.'

'Well move it then. Go on, get inside so I can tidy up the mess you lot always leave in the playground.'

Lee wondered if this was a trick. 'So ... I can go then?'

'You'd better, don't you think? And be quick about it, or else you'll be in as much trouble for being late as you would have been for not finishing your homework on time.'

'Right.'

Lee slung his bags over his shoulder, but a second later heard the sound of wrappers and their contents hitting the ground.

'What's this?' Jani Tor demanded.

Lee turned to see that he'd forgotten to fasten the top

of his schoolbag and, in pulling it onto his back, had thrown several bars of chocolate from it. He was mortified. However, he was also a quick thinker.

'I'm going with my Mum to visit some friends after school and she asked me to take some chocolate for them because it wouldn't fit in her handbag.'

'You've got a fair bit there.'

'Yeah, it's a huge family. There are fifteen children.'

'Fifteen!'

'Yeah. They don't have a television either.'

Jani Tor opened her eyes wide. 'That comes as no sur - prise whatsoever.'

Lee had no idea what she was on about. 'I'd better get going.'

'Yes, yes. On you go.'

Jani Tor walked off, muttering, 'Fifteen children … Fifteen! Imagine that …' while Lee ran, holding the top of his bag closed and zipping it up properly as soon as he was inside. He'd been lucky to escape the clutches of Panface's top spy. One look inside his schoolbag and the game would have been up.

Chapter
Seventeen

Uncle Raymond phoned Lee's mum to say he would be dropping by at the end of the week on his way to a meeting. This was potentially good news for Lee because his tuck shop stock was running low. He'd been down to the greenhouse to check what he had left and the answer was: not much. He needed to pay another visit to the cash and carry, and soon, otherwise he'd be left with nothing to sell.

Lee's dad was out late again. Lee waited until his mum was bathing Rebecca before phoning Uncle Raymond back. He spoke quickly and quietly so he wouldn't be heard, asking Uncle Raymond if he would mind stopping at the cash and carry on his way and picking up several more boxes of edible goodies.

'I've got plenty of money to pay you back with,' he told his uncle.

'That's good. Is business going well then?'

Lee told him how it had taken off in a big way.

'Blimey. Sounds like the supermarket chains had better watch out. Good for you. Do I take it that Mum and Dad still don't know?'

'Correct. I will tell them, only not just yet. Maybe in another month or so, once I'm more established. I'll probably need to by then, otherwise I won't be able to buy more stock. It's just lucky that you're coming to see us this week.'

'Uncle Raymond to the rescue, eh?'

'Something like that.'

'Okay, well I'll see you in a few days time.'

Lee hung up. He could tell from the singing upstairs that Rebecca was still in the bath.

It was true what he'd said about telling his parents. Uncle Raymond had been incredibly helpful so far, but Lee couldn't rely on him passing every few weeks. Normally they were lucky to see each other three or four times in a whole year.

The other point Lee needed to consider was the sheer volume of stock he would need to buy. The first time he'd had a few boxes that he could quickly run round the back with. But there was only so much room in the greenhouse, especially if he didn't want anyone to know what was in there. (And as greenhouses are made of glass, it's not too difficult to see through them.) Everything had to be squeezed in under the shelves if it was to remain hidden from prying eyes.

It was a lot to worry about. However, Lee shrugged it off as just one of those things that entrepreneurs have to deal with.

Chapter
Eighteen

The next weekend brought relief from school and some fantastic weather. It also meant Holly Arthanthou's car needed washed again.

Lee peeled off his sweaty T-shirt. As well as cooling you down, going shirtless had the added advantage that it didn't matter how much water you splashed about during car-washing, it was only your skin that got wet, not your clothes.

By now Lee had car-washing down to a fine art. He started with the windows because it made sense to wash them with clean water. Next he moved to the roof and worked his way down from there. Water from the roof soaked the muck on the rest of the car as it ran towards the ground. That made life easier when it came to cleaning the car's sides, bonnet and rear. He always left the wheels until last because they were usually dirty with brake dust as well as grime. If you were to wash them first you would be left with a bucket of black water that would make the rest of the car more filthy than it was to start with.

Holly commended him for his thoroughness and professionalism.

'I'll certainly recommend you to all my friends,' Holly told Lee, which would have been great news if only she'd actually had some friends.

It was almost lunchtime before Lee finished washing Holly's car. By then, the temperature had risen several more degrees. Across the road, Al Satian had inflated a paddling pool for his kids. Rogan had shown an initial interest in the sudden appearance of a pool of water in the middle of the garden, but had returned to the safety of the space under the kitchen table after Al's two young children had decided Rogan needed a bath. They hadn't been able to lift him into the paddling pool, but they had been able to fill buckets with water and empty them over him. It was amazing how skinny a dog could appear when soaked to the skin.

Lee decided to have a rest. He'd been working incred-ibly hard over the last few weeks and felt he deserved some time out. He grabbed a comic and unrolled a blanket onto the grass outside the back door.

He still had the idea that he would expand into selling comics, but had decided to leave that for at least another month, until after he'd told his parents what he was doing with his mobile tuck shop and how successful it was. Once they knew just how well he'd done in so short a time, they would, he was sure, finally agree to help him in his enterprise. It would be in their own best interests, because if Lee became a multi-zillionaire he would be able to look after them in their old age. And that time wasn't far off, because they had both turned forty already.

Rebecca came out of the house and lay next to him on the rug. She pretended to read Lee's comic, but her interest in it didn't last. After that she climbed onto Lee's back and told him to 'gee up'.

'Rebecca, why can't you be like a normal girl and play with dolls instead of jumping all over me?'

Rebecca didn't answer. Instead, she tickled Lee's sides.

'I'm not tickly,' Lee told her.

'You are.'

'I'm not.'

'You are.'

He was. And now Rebecca got him right where he was tickliest: under his arms. Lee squirmed like a squid then bucked like a bronco, sending Rebecca flying through the air. He couldn't help it. When he was tickled he lost all control of himself.

Rebecca landed in a heap on the grass. A second later she was up again and ready for more action. Lee leapt up, too, and ran off down the garden, with Rebecca chasing him.

After a minute Rebecca decided it was time to change the order of things. 'It's your turn to chase me,' she instructed.

'Okay,' Lee agreed. He allowed her a few steps head start then set off after her. Rebecca couldn't run as fast as him, but her shorter legs and lighter weight meant she was able to stop, turn and change direction more quickly, making it surprisingly difficult to catch her.

Lee was enjoying himself. He chased Rebecca up to the house, then back down the garden again, twice. On the second occasion Rebecca decided she would evade Lee by escaping INTO THE GREENHOUSE.

'No!' Lee shouted. But Rebecca didn't stop, she started to slide behind the bashed and broken piece of fence that lay across the greenhouse's entrance.

'Rebecca, stop! The greenhouse is about to fall down!'

That halted Rebecca in her tracks. But after a second looking at it she said, 'No it's not.'

'No, no, it's really really dangerous. Dad said to tell you that it could fall down at any moment and if it did then the glass would probably cut you in half and kill you. So you must stay away from the greenhouse.'

'Dad didn't say that.'

'He did.'

'Didn't.'

'Did.'

'Didn't.'

'He did, Rebecca. And he said he would never forgive himself if anything happened to either of us. He would be heartbroken and would have to run away somewhere.'

'Where?'

'Somewhere far away.'

'Like Wales?'

'Yes, maybe as far away as that.'

Rebecca hadn't moved. And, much more importantly, she hadn't noticed what was in the greenhouse.

'Now, Rebecca, come back out again, very carefully, okay?'

Rebecca looked closely at the greenhouse again. 'Why's it dangerous?'

'Because, eh, the metal frame is...rusted. And so is the glass. Yes, it's all very rusty because the greenhouse is so old. One touch and it could all come crashing down. Honestly, you've got to come away from it.'

Rebecca moved reluctantly towards him. 'You just want to catch me.'

Lee waited until she was within striking distance, then grabbed her. 'No I didn't! But I've got you anyway!'

The episode with Rebecca and the greenhouse had been a close shave, even though Lee was too young to have bristles on his chin. No harm had been done by it, however it emphasised to Lee that he would soon need a long-term solution to his storage needs. The problem was his parents. Telling them was no more appealing than it had ever been. They had been so staunchly opposed to him becoming involved in the tuck shop enterprise to start with that even if he could convince them he'd made a success of it, they might nevertheless ban him from continuing.

It took Lee a long time to fall asleep that night because he couldn't help but worry about his predicament. If he were forced to close his mobile tuck shop, the fall from grace would be unbearable. He would tumble from being a contender for Businessman of the Year one day to being Lee the Nobody (again) the next. What would the other kids at school think? After years of ignoring him most of them at least now knew who he was.

It was better not to be a somebody in the first place than to slide from being a somebody to being a nobody. He could imagine the reaction of kids like Craig the Creepoid. They would slag him off ('What happened to your business empire, Lee? Did it go bust?') and then forget about him as they returned to buying their tuck from Panface's shop. Worse still, a fellow pupil might steal his idea and carry on from where he would be forced to leave off. That really would be dreadful.

Lee wished he could speak to someone else about his concerns, but the truth was that there was only Will, and he didn't seem interested in the mobile tuck shop anymore. And it didn't take a genius to recognise that all the other kids at school were more interested in the contents of Lee's tuck shop bags than in him as a person.

Chapter
Nineteen

At first when Lee woke up he couldn't work out why. Then he remembered.

It had started as a dream. He'd been upstairs in his bedroom when the doorbell had rung. His mum had answered the door, but, as is sometimes the way with dreams, Lee could see what was going on at the doorstep even though he was still in his room. It was Will wanting to know if Lee wanted to hang out. Lee's mum said no, he was too busy being an entrepreneur, but thanked Will for asking. Will wasn't as surprised as Lee expected. 'No problem, I've got a new best friend anyway,' he said.

That was what had woken Lee so suddenly.

A new best friend? It couldn't be. He and Will had been best friends since the day they'd started school. What could possibly change that now?

Maybe it was Asad. Maybe he had turned Will against him. It didn't seem likely, because Lee's limited experience of Asad was that he was one of life's good guys, but Lee could think of no other explanation. It was true that Lee and Will hadn't seen much of each other recently, but that couldn't possibly have destroyed their close friendship

...could it?

Of course, it was only a dream, nothing more. Just some silly combination of thoughts floating into his head in the middle of the night. He shouldn't be paying any attention to it because he and Will would always be as close as two goldfish in a egg cup.

Still, it was difficult to put it out of his mind altogether.

Fortunately it was a brilliant, bright, sunny summer's day, which lifted Lee's spirits no end. The sun always had an uplifting effect on him.

This particular bright, sunny summer's morning was a Monday. And Monday mornings meant school again.

It was never much fun heading off to school in the morning, but it was even worse when you knew you were going to be missing out on a sunny day.

The sun hadn't stopped shining all weekend. It had been roasting, so hot that Lee's mum had insisted on smearing him and Rebecca with greasy suntan lotion. ('Well it's better than getting skin cancer,' she kept saying. Lee supposed that, for once, she was right.)

But there was no need for suntan lotion on a Monday morning, even if it was sunny, because there was no danger of getting a tan inside Lee's classroom. You might get hot and bothered as rays streamed in through the filthy windows, but your skin wasn't going to darken. Nor was it going to flake off in sheets the size of bath towels, which was a shame because it was rather good fun to pick at when it was like that. You could even chew on bits as you stripped them off, but it was best not to tell anyone about that in case they thought you'd become a cannibal.

Still, at least Monday meant Lee could open his mobile tuck shop again, and so continue his journey on the road to fame and fortune.

So he set off on his regular route: out of the front door, down the path, and into the track that ran along behind his family's house. However, he'd taken no more than eight steps into the track before he stopped dead.

A rubbish bin had moved. It had moved even though no-one was near it.

He was sure of it. He had good eyesight, unlike his dad, and he had definitely seen the bin rock and then slide a few inches to one side.

He knew whose bin it was too. A big number **66** was painted on the front, which meant it was from the house in the street behind theirs where an old couple lived. As he stood transfixed, Lee realised what must have happened. The old people had been duped by a smooth-talking spy for Panface who had persuaded them that, in the interests of national security, he or she needed to take over their rubbish bin and use it in an important operation. He or she had then equipped the bin with hi-tech surveillance equipment, using the circles of the two '6's to disguise the ends of the tiny cameras, and placed it opposite the very spot where Lee collected his stash of stock each morning. They wanted to catch him in the act, to make sure they had video evidence the police could use to have him locked him up in jail for many years to come.

He had to think quickly, which wasn't easy so early in the morning, especially after a poor night's sleep.

And then he had a brainwave.

It wasn't much of a brainwave, but it wasn't bad for that time of day. Lee bent forward, raised his hands to his head and made as much of a mess of his hair as he possibly could. He tried to make it seem as if he'd had to leave home first before he could do this – as if his parents would strongly disapprove of him attending school so scruffily.

This didn't solve the problem of what to do next or how he was going to get to his stock, but it provided some much-needed thinking time.

He back-tracked up the lane and, at the end of it, headed up the road as if on his way to school. Five minutes later, having walked around the block, he entered the lane from the other end, thankful that his eagle eyes had allowed him to spot the movement of the green bin. It was obviously remote controlled, but as the bin's wheels hadn't been tampered with (at least as far as he could tell) it would only be able to move backwards and forwards, not sideways. Knowing that it wouldn't be able to turn, Lee confidently marched towards it. He became less confident as he neared it, but carried on, watching for the slightest movement. He stopped once he was about five metres away. His nerve was failing him. What if the bin wasn't remote-controlled? What if someone was actually in it?

Lee took a big breath, then ... another. And one more, just for good luck. Then pounced.

What did he have to lose? If there was someone in the bin then they probably already had some idea of what he was up to. But it would take them a good few seconds to climb out of the bin, valuable time in which Lee would be able to escape ... although he had no idea where he might escape to.

'Asha!' he cried as he leapt forward at the bin. It was the

sort of cry his Taekwondo instructor used, designed to scare the enemy. Much the same as the Scots who played bagpipes before charging, making enemies think they were skinning cats with their bare hands as practice for what they'd do during battle.

And scare his enemy Lee did. He quickly lifted the lid of the bin. As it rose there was a terrifying screech, as if a cat had been scared witless and was making a break for it.

Which was quite a coincidence, because at that precise moment a large cat leapt from the bin, knocking it over, and shot off down the lane towards the road (where hopefully it obeyed the Green Cross Code and didn't get run over).

Lee was twenty or thirty metres down the lane before his brain allowed him to stop fleeing and start thinking again.

Wow, that had been scary. Not just scary, but Scary Hairy Mary, because Hairy Mary was the name of the pensioners' stupid cat. She was one of those big puffballs, the sort that look as if they've been blow-dried.

Lee allowed himself to look back as he slowed. Behind him the bin was on its side, knocked flying by the escaping moggy, revealing that it was now empty apart from something small at the bottom of it. Relieved that his secret was still safe, Lee stole cautiously back up the lane, his eyes scanning everything around him but never leaving the thing in the bottom of the bin for long.

He was about three metres away before he realised what it was.

A dead mouse. A dead mouse that had been rather well chewed.

When the bins were collected they were often left open, so presumably the cat must have jumped in then. But how the lid had closed was a mystery. Maybe someone had done it for a laugh. If so, it wasn't funny, not just for the poor cat (and even less so for the mouse), but also for Lee. He was still shaking. The cat had given him a huge fright. A huge, big, massive, ginormous fright.

But there was no time for feeling terrified. A glance at his watch revealed that Lee had just twenty minutes left to stock up and get to school. He'd already missed a fair bit of his pre-school selling time and needed to crack on.

He pushed open the rickety gate at the bottom of his family's garden and crept towards the greenhouse.

The trees, shrubs, flowers and weeds (and there were a lot of the last category in his family's garden) had all grown substantially in the two months since he'd started visiting there each morning. Now there was no chance of his mother seeing him from any of the windows at the back of the house as he stocked up. And, even better, the extra greenery meant he could safely store more stock because the greenhouse's sides were more effectively screened.

The bit of fencing was there in its usual place. Lee slid it to one side and squeezed by it. The heat attacked him as he entered. The air in the greenhouse was parched. Lee waved his arms around, trying to generate some sort of breeze.

Everything appeared to be in place. Lee looked about, deciding what stock he ought to pack. He had plenty of choice now that Uncle Raymond had delivered the new batch of grub. He decided to start by loading up a bundle of ordinary chocolate bars. One of Creepy Craig's cohorts was partial to them, as was Idle Ian (though of course there wasn't much Idle Ian wasn't partial to).

Lee found the relevant cardboard box and ripped open the top, using his thumbnail to slice through the tape that held down the flaps. Opening a fresh box was still special to Lee, revealing the rows of bars, all neatly lined up like soldiers on parade, and knowing that those bars were several layers deep. It reminded him that these weren't sweets he'd bought with his pocket money. No, these were the basis of his business empire. One day those boxes would contain layers and layers of gold bars. And they would all be his.

Lee peeled back the flaps of the box, stuck a hand in and picked out a bundle of bars to stick in one of his tuck shop bags.

At that precise moment, as he held the bars, Lee wished more than ever that they were made of gold. Not because that would mean he was very rich and could retire to a large villa in a hot country (though it certainly would mean that); and not because he would be able to buy all the things he'd ever dreamed of, like a quad bike and a remote control racing car (though that was also true). No, the reason it would have been good if those bars had been made of gold had much more to do with another difference between gold bars and chocolate.

Gold is a heavy yellow metal. It is found in thin gaps between rocks. Most gold comes from South Africa, the USA and parts of Russia. Together those countries produce about 1,100 tonnes of gold every year. That sounds a lot, but remember that a square of gold is much heavier than a square of chocolate of the same size. You could store a tonne of gold bars in something the size of a schoolbag because each one is so heavy, whereas you'd need a space the size of a garage to store a tonne of chocolate bars.

A bar of chocolate may seem expensive, but try buying a bar of gold next time you're out at the shops. If you do, take a lot of money with you, or a very rich old relative who has lost their marbles and won't realise just how much of their money you're spending. Gold is expensive. Extremely expensive. It's extremely expensive because there isn't all that much of it about, especially given how much we like to wear it.

But none of this explains why it would have been much better if those bars of chocolate in the box Lee had just opened had been made of gold instead of chocolate.

Nor does the fact that gold is long lasting and easy to shape. (It's malleable, if you want a posh word for it.) Or that it is more highly resistant to acids than most metals. Or even that it would break your customers' teeth were they to chew it.

No, there's one thing that gold is particularly good at that chocolate isn't, and that's coping with a lot of heat. Sure, gold will eventually melt, but only at quite a high temperature. Even then, when it cools down it will still be gold.

Chocolate is rather different. Expose chocolate to a high temperature and you know what will happen: it will melt. And, when it melts, the different ingredients – the sugar, the milk and the cocoa – separate out. The result: a horrible, gooey, sticky yuckiness that hardens to a brown and white mess; one which customers would complain bitterly about if you sold it to them.

This was the nightmare realisation that hit Lee as he scooped up his handful of chocolate bars. The bars were soft. They were mushy. They were slumping in his hand like the leaves of a plant that hasn't had water for weeks. And the bars were squidgy. Very very squidgy indeed.

Lee peeled back the wrapper of one bar and revealed his worst fear: the entire surface of the bar had disintegrated into a layer of brown stickiness. 'Oh no!' he moaned.

This was a disaster. He threw the rest of the packs back into their box and ripped open a different one, desperately hoping the sun hadn't affected the whole of the greenhouse, just a bit of it – that something, somewhere might have survived. But it was the same story. Every piece of confectionery he'd bought had at least a chocolate covering, and so every piece had melted.

Lee slumped onto a nearly empty box of crisps. It was

unable to bear his weight, so he fell straight into it, crushing the remaining bags and causing one or two of them to explode. His head dropped into his hands. What had he been thinking? Greenhouses exist to protect plants from cold in winter and give them extra heat in summer. Had his stock needed protection from the cold? No. Had it needed added heat? Definitely not.

He hadn't even considered temperature when he'd decided to use the greenhouse. He'd used it because it had been his only option. Where else could he have stored his stock without his parents finding it?

But still, he was annoyed and frustrated with himself. He should have foreseen what would happen. It was no excuse that when he'd started up his mobile tuck shop it had been earlier in the year and the temperatures had been nothing like those the country was now experiencing. The clocks had sprung forward and summer had arrived, and with it had come a mini heatwave. The sun had risen progressively higher in the sky so that the leaves of the garden's big sycamore tree no longer protected the greenhouse's glass panes.

What was he going to do now? Come morning break, or even earlier, his regular customers would be queuing up to buy from him, and what would he have to offer? Crisps.

Nothing else, just crisps. And some of those were now smashed to smithereens.

With his free hand, Lee wiped away the sweat that the stifling heat had caused to form on his brow. An image came to him of Wayne Scales shaking his head in disappointment and disbelief at Lee's stupidity. He'd made such a mess of his once-promising business enterprise. From nothing to success and back to nothing again, all within a couple of months.

He was a failure.

Lee's watch told him that the school bell was due to ring in less than ten minutes. But how could he go to school? He would be a laughing stock, the butt of everyone's jokes.

He considered spending the whole day in the greenhouse and pretending to his schoolmates that he was ill, but that would only delay the inevitable. In any case, it was boiling. If he remained there much longer he would pass out from heat exhaustion.

Lee gazed through his splayed fingers at the boxes that surrounded him. He'd spent a fortune on the ruined stock. He'd sunk every penny he'd earned into it.

The realisation of how much the mistake had cost him only served to make Lee even more despondent. 'You idiot,' he berated himself. 'Why didn't you think?!'

Another few minutes passed. Decision time was drawing near. If he waited much longer he would be late for school. But that was the least of his worries.

'What would you do, Mr Scales?' Lee mumbled.

Wayne Scales didn't answer, not surprisingly given that he wasn't there.

But it made Lee think. What *would* Mr Scales do?

Well, for a start he wouldn't give up. Imagination and attitude, hadn't those been the two attributes he'd said distinguished a great entrepreneur from the crowd of average Joes? And didn't Lee have both of those attributes?

He did. So why wasn't he using them? There had to be a way out of this mess. He was suddenly sure of it. If only he could think what it was.

Chapter
Twenty

Logic suggested there were only three things Lee could do with his ruined stock: dump it, sell it or eat it. Normally the last of these would have been the most tempting, but the morning's disasters had put Lee right off food. Plus, he'd be sick if he ate the amount in question.

Dumping it would be a terrible waste, especially as there was nothing actually wrong with the chocolate – well, nothing that would kill anyone – it was just discoloured.

He could sell it at a discount as slightly spoiled seconds. That would at least get him some of his money back.

Or he could say nothing at all and hope to get away with it …

Hmm. Tempting.

Very tempting.

Very very tempting.

About as tempting as if the owner of a sweetshop asked you to mind the place while he nipped out for a two-hour lunch, saying, 'If you get hungry, just help yourself.'

Very very very very tempting.

But also very very very very wrong. It would get him out of one hole but drop him straight into another. He would be able to sell his stock, but when his customers opened the wrappers they would realise they'd been diddled and would immediately want their money back. And, more importantly, it would be the last time they bought from him. No, selling the stock that way would bring about the irreversible closure of *Lee's Mobile Tuck Shop*, and he wasn't prepared to concede that. Not without a fight, anyway.

Lee's imagination had woken up now. Another thought struck him. He could nip round to Panface's shop, buy a load of stock from there and take it to school to sell while he worked out how to get more stock of his own. That wouldn't make him any money because he would only be able to sell for about the same price as he was able to purchase it from Panface, but it would buy him time. And maybe, in the meantime, he could fool the wholesalers into believing that the stock had melted at their premises, before it had been delivered to him, in which case he ought to be able to get all his money back.

It was an interesting idea, but it had three drawbacks. Firstly, he would have to buy such large quantities from Panface that he would arouse the ugly shopkeeper's suspicions, and that could lead to him speaking to the school, finding out about *Lee's Mobile Tuck Shop* and having it closed permanently. Secondly, he didn't have any cash with which to pay Panface because it was all tied up in his stock. And thirdly, the wholesalers were unlikely to believe him, as indeed Lee wouldn't believe any of his customers if they came to him with such a story.

Still, a little more encouraged by having finally come up with at least a few ideas, Lee decided to face school. He stuffed his bags with as much grub as usual, just in case a flash of inspiration came to him before the morning interval. Better to be prepared than not, even if the grub was still as soft as Plasticine.

Lee hurried along and made the end of the queue at the school doors seconds before The Ogre appeared.

'I see you're last, Lee,' she said severely. 'But at least you're here. Not that that's a cause for celebration.'

The morning started with project work. Their current subject was Italy. They had covered the basics over the last two weeks: where Italy is (in Southern Europe, sticking out into the Mediterranean Sea), how big it is (301,000 square kilometres), how many people live there (57 million, about the same as the UK) and what it makes its money from (wine – it produces more than any other country in the world – cars, textiles and leather goods). This morning they were focusing on what Italy was famous for.

'Footballers!' Liam called out.

'That's right,' The Ogre said, 'though don't shout out. Put your hand up first. Now, what can you tell us about their footballers?'

'They're a bunch of dirty hackers,' Liam told her. 'But some of them are good strikers and score loads of goals.'

'Right. Interesting.' She addressed the whole class. 'What else is it famous for? Yes, Hannah.'

'The Leaning Tower of Pizza.'

'Pisa,' The Ogre corrected. 'The Leaning Tower of Pisa, not Pizza. I don't think a tower made of dough and top-pings would last very long, do you?'

'The birds would eat it,' Lee suggested. 'Or it would cook in the sun and the tourists would munch it.'

'Yes, Lee. Very good,' The Ogre said sarcastically.

'Now then, Hannah, what more serious information can you tell us about the Leaning Tower of Pisa?'

'Eh, the builders were rubbish?'

'Well ...'

'They must have been, because the Tower's leaning over and nearly falling down. The builders must have been a bunch of cowboys.'

'I didn't know they had cowboys in Italy,' said Arthur, a particularly thick classmate of Lee's. 'Is that why you get spaghetti westerns?'

The Ogre ignored Arthur and addressed Hannah. 'Yes, you're quite right that it leans over a fair bit, but that's because of the unstable ground it's built on. Now, has anyone else got something intelligent to contribute? What else is Italy famous for? Yes, Simone?'

'Marble.'

'Oh well done, Simone. That's a very interesting one.'

The Ogre was always nice to Simone. She never shouted at her like she did at other kids - Lee, for instance. Simone's parents were rich and the other kids all reckoned The Ogre was hoping for a present of more than an apple at the end of the school year. Plus, Simone's dad was a school governor and it was obvious that The Ogre didn't want any bad reports going back to him.

'We've got some marble round our fireplace,' Simone said. 'Daddy said it was very expensive, which is why we're not allowed to walk on it.'

'Oh, it *is* expensive! Very expensive. You're lucky to have some. And can anyone else tell me what marble looks like?'

Caleb had his hand up and The Ogre pointed at him. 'It's very polished and has different colours through it sometimes. Sort of streaky and swirly.'

'Yes, Caleb, you're right. Pure marble is white and is a

form of limestone, but very often you get impurities in it, and those are what give it the swirling patterns you often see.'

Lee didn't normally enjoy project work, but this time he had a feeling it might just save his skin.

Chapter
Twenty-One

'Hey, Ian!'

Idle Ian turned and walked towards Lee, who was already walking towards him. They met in the middle.

'Yes, please,' Ian said before Lee had opened either of the bags he was carrying.

Lee was confused. 'But I haven't told you what I'm offering.'

'I know, but whatever it is, I'll take some.'

This was welcome – if predictable – news to Lee.

'What I was going to say to you was that I've got a special treat for you today.'

'A special treat?' Idle Ian was doubly interested. 'What is it?'

'I've managed to get this special range of chocolate that's normally only sold in Italy. The Italians are going mad for it, so it was extremely difficult to get hold of. I managed it this time by calling in a favour, however I very much doubt I'll be able to get any more.'

Lee took out a bar from one of his mobile tuck shop bags, glad the classroom had been a lot less warm than the greenhouse. It had given the chocolate a chance to solidify again. 'Now, this may look to you like a normal bar of chocolate, but once you open it up you'll see just how different it is. It has a special marble effect.'

'Does it taste any different, though?'

'Oh sure. You'll see when you open it that they have a special manufacturing process that mixes the cocoa, milk and sugar in a completely different way to what they do for our market. And what a difference it makes! My taste buds couldn't believe it when I tried a sample.'

'Is it more expensive?'

'In Italy it's *way* more expensive. But I'll tell you what, seeing as you're one of my regulars, I'll let you have it for the same price it costs me. That's still a bit more expensive than normal, but believe me, it's well worth it.'

'Cheers, Lee. Thanks.' Idle Ian rummaged about in his pockets and produced the same mountain of change that he always seemed to carry. As he did so, Lee said, 'I suspect these special Italian bars will sell out in next to no time. I haven't told anyone else about them yet, I decided to give you first chance at buying them.'

'Right, I'll have four, then,' Idle Ian declared.

'Four ...' Lee couldn't believe his luck. He added a few pence to the normal cost of each bar and then announced the total. Idle Ian didn't bat an eyelid. He even took two packets of crisps as well.

It took quite an effort for Lee not to grin too widely as Idle Ian walked off. Not only had Lee sold some melted stock, he'd actually managed to sell it for more than usual! He was a genius salesman. Mr Scales would be proud of him. He'd used his imagination, coupled with his never-say-die attitude, to come up with a fantastic idea for getting himself out of the very big hole the heat of the greenhouse had burned for him.

And now another potential customer was walking towards him. So with renewed confidence he introduced the next mug to his new luxury Italian range of marbled confectionery.

Lee's fellow pupils lapped up his story and munched down mouthfuls of the marbled chocolate. Lee had discovered a well-known business principle: tell people that something is rare and they'll want more of it. The trick wasn't to have something that was rare, but to make people think you did – to make it seem exclusive instead of ordinary.

Even Will was interested. 'How did you get hold of it?' he asked. 'I didn't know you had contacts in Italy. Do you know a Mafia smuggler or something?'

Lee wasn't sure how to answer without lying, so instead he said, 'Aha! That's my little secret.'

Lee and Will had been seeing less and less of each other. Lee was simply too busy, and Will was hanging out with Asad most of the time. It had started off with Will showing Asad around after he'd moved to their school, but now they walked to and from school together and spent the intervals chatting or playing. About the only time Lee did see Will these days was when Will joined Lee's queue of customers. Even then they didn't have long to talk.

'Asad and I are going swimming tomorrow after school,' Will said quickly, knowing how much of a rush Lee was always in. 'Do you want to come?'

'I'd love to.'

'Great!'

'But I can't.'

'Oh. Why not?'

'I've got to tidy Upa Blin Dali's garden.'

'Couldn't you leave it until the weekend?'

Lee shook his head. 'I won't have time. I've got Holly Arthanthou's car to wash then, and Rogan to walk. Plus, I'll need to sort out my stock.'

'What needs sorting out about it?'

'It's …' Lee almost gave the game away. 'Eh, it's complicated getting hold of this Italian stuff. I have to see if I can get some more.' Lee turned his attention back to his other customers. 'Next!'

Will didn't move off immediately. He stood his ground a moment and said, 'You know, Lee, you've become so obsessed with this business thing that you've forgotten who your friends are. Or who they used to be.'

And then, without waiting for a reply, Will turned and joined Asad, who was standing nearby.

Chapter
Twenty-Two

Walking Rogan was the only part of the day when Lee could be guaranteed time to himself. Well, obviously Rogan was with him, but he was a dog, not a human, and although he had needs, none of them involved conversation.

Lee had put to the back of his mind Will's comment in the playground about forgetting who his friends were. There had been more important things to concentrate on, such as passing off melted stock as specialist Italian marble chocolate. But now that he had no customers in front of him to concentrate on, Will's comments returned to him. What had inspired such a barbed remark? Was Will jealous of Lee's new-found wealth? Was Lee's drive and ambition making Will feel inadequate and ordinary? Maybe they were both just growing up at different speeds, with Lee maturing more quickly than Will. It was something his mum said often happened.

Lee couldn't help it if he was determined to succeed. There was nothing wrong with the desire to do well. But however much he tried to shrug off Will's comments they kept coming back to him. They were hurtful. Lee didn't think of himself as obsessive. Well, not unhealthily so. You needed a bit of obsession to do well in anything; without it you'd give up as soon as a problem arose. However, that didn't mean he'd forgotten who his best friend was. He was just...finding it difficult to set aside as much time for him as before.

Lee had been very tempted by Will's suggestion that they should go swimming. Lee loved swimming. Until recently he had gone whenever he could, especially since they'd reopened the pool after installing an amazingly ginormous flume. It was brilliant, particularly the fast bit near the middle when you flew up the sides as if you were in a toboggan at the Winter Olympics, haring down a course carved from the snow and ice of a mountainside.

Rogan stopped to sniff a gatepost and Lee allowed the lead to fall slack.

The more Lee thought about swimming, the more he wanted to go to the pool. He hadn't had any fun for quite a while. So he tried to work out if he could rearrange his busy diary to make time, if not for the sake of going swimming then at least for the sake of his friendship with Will. After all, what would he do during the school holidays if Will no longer wanted to hang around with him? There was a real danger that the only person available to play with him would be his sister, Rebecca. Cute as she was in small doses, Lee didn't relish the prospect of spending the whole summer with her and her doll-loving friends.

And maybe Will had a point. Even Wayne Scales had to relax. What would be the point of having a swimming pool at his mansion if he never swam in it? Surely there ought to be more to life than work, work, work. That was slavery. Okay, it was certainly better to be a slave to your own ambitions than to be a slave to someone else's, but the end result was the same: all work and no play.

Having had a good sniff, Rogan now cocked his leg and left his mark on the gatepost.

Chapter
Twenty-Three

Lee held the telephone handset to his ear.

'Hello?' said a voice at the other end of the line. It was Will's mum.

'Hi, it's Lee. Can I speak to Will, please?'

'Lee! We haven't heard from you for ages. I was beginning to think that you, too, had disappeared off the face of the earth. As you know, extinction is a terrible fate that's already befallen a great many animal species on Earth.'

Will's mum was big into environmentalism. Or maybe just mentalism, because she could be a bit odd at times. She wore old clothes. At least, that's what they looked like; if they were new then she either had terrible fashion sense or bought all her clothes from a shopkeeper who, like Lee, knew a sucker when he met one and had the skill to sell dodgy, knackered stock to them. And she had long straggly hair, not at all like the glossy sort newsreaders sported. Will's mum went on marches at which she held aloft placards, protesting against the various ways mankind was destroying the planet. She had been in the local newspaper on several occasions. Will had been rather embarrassed by her antics, even though he thought they were for a good cause.

'I've been really busy,' Lee told her. 'I've got a couple of jobs.'

'So I've heard. Busy, busy, busy, that's what I've heard you are.'

'Yes, that's right.' News of his success had obviously reached Will's parents. 'Is Will in?'

'He's gone out with Asad. You've just missed them.'

'Aw.'

'Will said he'd asked if you wanted to go, but he seemed to think you weren't interested – that you had more important things to do.'

'Well, I'm, eh …'

'Busy? I'm sure you are, but I know Will's disappointed you two don't hang out any more.'

'Yeah. Me too.'

'Oh, that's good. Is there any particular reason why we haven't seen you around recently? I keep asking Will if you two have fallen out and he keeps telling me "no".'

'He's right, we haven't fallen out.'

'So what's stopping you, then?'

'I've just been working really hard all the time.'

'All rest and no play makes Jack a dull boy,' Will's mum said.

'Who's Jack? What's he got to do with it?'

'It's just a saying.'

'Aw.'

'Anyway, if you're still interested, you could probably catch up with them if you're quick. They only left a few minutes ago, and if they're chatting as much as usual then they won't have walked far.'

'Okay, thanks.'

Lee didn't hang around after putting the phone down. Catching up with Will and Asad became the sole purpose in his life. As he dashed around the house, collecting a towel and swimming shorts and throwing them into the first bag that came to hand (a plastic one with a tear in the side, but he didn't care), he called out to his mum where he was heading and with whom.

Once out of the front gate he looked down the hill. There was no sign of Will and Asad, so he broke into a jog that developed into a run as the steep slope carried him along ever faster. His legs ran away from him and he was almost unable to stop when he reached the first road. He was forced to grab hold of a lamppost to save himself. A surprised-but-alert driver slammed his brakes on. Inside the car the man shouted and waved his arms and formed his fingers into certain well-known unfriendly shapes. Lee understood what the shapes meant (and it wasn't 'hello' or 'good to see you'), but considered the man's shouting pointless because the car windows were closed and Lee couldn't hear him. Mind you, that was probably just as well.

Lee was more careful after that. Three corners later his closest friend, and his closest friend's new closest friend, were in sight, dawdling along, each with a bag slung over their shoulder.

Lee increased his speed. Then, when he was within 50 metres of them, he called out, 'Hey, wait for me!'

Will and Asad stopped and turned around, then looked at each other. Lee kept running. He was close enough now that he could see the surprise on Will's face. A few seconds later it changed to a grin.

'What are you doing here?' Will asked rather coolly.

'Can I come swimming with you?'

Will looked at Asad and shrugged. 'I don't see why not. But I thought you were too busy.'

'Well, I haven't really seen you properly for a while, so I thought I'd come along.'

'What about all your other stuff? What about walking Rogan?'

'Already done.'

'That was quick.'

'Dad says that the busier you are the quicker you get things done.'

'He's probably right.'

'Yeah.' There was a strange silence between them. There'd never been one of those before. 'I've also missed hanging around with you,' Lee admitted to Will. 'I've been a bit too, you know ...'

'Obsessive?' Will tried.

'Well, yeah, a bit.'

'You've been running your mobile tuck shop, right?' Asad asked.

Lee nodded. 'Running my tuck shop, cleaning cars, digging gardens, walking dogs and forgetting about my friends.' Lee looked to Will. 'Sorry about that.'

'Don't worry about it,' Will said. 'I'll probably do the same some day.'

'Thanks.'

'Have you two been friends forever?' Asad asked.

'A bit longer than that,' Will told him.

'Yeah, since Roman times,' Lee said.

'That's a long time. You must both be ancient.'

'Not us,' Lee said. 'That's our parents you're thinking of.'

Asad was a brilliant swimmer, much better than either Lee or Will.

'My dad taught me to start with, then I joined a club for a while. If you think I'm good, you should have seen some of the others there. They swam like dolphins.'

Maybe. But Asad was still extremely quick through the water, which made catching him in swimming-pool tig almost impossible.

They had been at the pool for over two hours when finally Asad said he needed to head home.

It was only once they were all out of the water that Lee realised how tired his body was. 'I'm cream crackered,' he said.

'Me, too,' Will told him. 'It's the water. It helps support your body when you're in it, but that makes you feel as if you've doubled in weight when you come out.'

It was true, and it made for a slow journey home as they placed one weary leg in front of the other, especially up the hill to Lee's house.

'That was great,' Lee told Will and Asad. 'Let's go again sometime soon.'

'How about the same time next week?' Asad suggested.

'I'm up for it,' Will said. He looked to Lee to see what he would say.

'Me, too,' Lee agreed without hesitating. 'I'm going to start enjoying myself more again.'

Will didn't say anything. He didn't need to. His toothy smile said it for him.

Chapter
Twenty-Four

Lee lay in bed, thinking. The light was out, which made thinking easier even though it made staying awake more difficult.

The light being out meant there were no other distractions. Lee couldn't see any toys, books or posters. He wasn't tempted to imagine that the shadows thrown by the light hanging in the middle of his room were ghosts or mutants. And there was no point in picking his nose because he wouldn't be able to see the size of the bogey before he flicked it in the general direction of the rubbish bin. (Most of his shots missed, so Lee never stood in that part of his room in his bare feet. Rather unfairly, he didn't warn others not to.)

Lee was thinking about how much he'd enjoyed the afternoon at the swimming pool with Will and Asad. Uncle Raymond often told him, 'You're only young once, so make the most of it'. Lee had, until now, thought it was just another one of his uncle's daft sayings, but now he was beginning to understand what it meant. There would be many years ahead of him when he'd have to slog his guts out at work, just like he did at school. So, in the meantime, he ought to have some fun. Fun was a good part of what made human life so special. Spiders and flies didn't have much fun, at least as far as Lee could tell. You certainly never heard them laughing out loud. 'Ha ha ha, I've fallen off my web and been flushed down the sink. What a laugh!' Or: 'Ha ha ha, I've been caught in the spider's web and now the eight-legged monster is coming to eat me from the inside out after first wrapping me up in loads of sticky stuff.' Okay, so monkeys and their like had fun, jumping around in trees or on rocks, but that was no surprise because they were very similar to humans. (And particularly similar to a few of Lee's classmates.) What was the point of being human if you didn't make the most of it? And if swimming gave you more pleasure than digging a garden or washing cars then you ought to make sure you made time for it. So Lee decided that, from now on, he would.

He'd been lucky (and just a teency weency bit devious) to have passed off all that melted cocoa, milk and sugar as fancy Italian marble-style chocolate. Next time something went wrong he might not be so fortunate. So it would be better if there wasn't a next time. He had made a profit already, enough to buy a few things he wanted. He ought to quit while he was ahead. Surely even Wayne Scales would agree with that. It was time to grab hold of happiness again. He would spend more time with Will (and Asad, too) and rebuild their friendship. That didn't mean he wouldn't do any work. He would still clean Holly Arthanthou's car, weed Upa Blin Dali's garden and walk Al Satian's dog. Half an hour to walk a dog and the same on a Saturday morning to wash a car was fine. And the gardening could be done anytime he wanted. But he would close down the tuck shop. That way he would have intervals and lunchtimes free – the times he used to spend with Will. Plus, closing down the mobile tuck shop would mean he wouldn't have to tell his parents that he'd gone behind their backs.

Lee drifted off into slumber, content with his new life plan.

Chapter
Twenty-Five

Within ten days Lee had sold most of the bars of chocolate and packets of crisps in his stock. Throughout that time he paid close attention to the weather forecast. Fortunately the temperature dropped and it even rained on a few of the days, so he didn't have to move what remained.

So that was it, no more *Lee's Mobile Tuck Shop*.

Which was just as well. Because the very next day Lee was heading out into the playground when he saw the misshapen face of someone coming in the opposite direction. Someone he recognised. Someone he didn't want to see within a mile of the school. His heart jumped. Other bits of his body did too, but it was his heart that he noticed most because it was the part keeping him alive.

It was Panface.

And he'd spotted Lee.

'Hoi!' he called as he stepped up to the school's main door.

'Eh, hello Pan ... Eh, I mean, hello there.' There was a quiver in Lee's voice.

'Which way to the head's office?'

'The headmistress's?'

'Yeah. The headmistress's.'

'Eh, it's that way.' Lee reluctantly pointed up the corridor. 'Visitors are meant to go to the office first.'

'Right.'

Lee had never seen Panface up at the school before. It was mid morning. Surely he ought to have been down at his shop serving whoever it was that went shopping in the middle of the morning. Old people. People on their way home from night shift. Mothers and fathers whose kids had gone off to school, leaving them in peace for a few hours. People who'd taken a day's holiday and had lain in bed until now. People who hadn't taken a day's holiday but who had lain in bed anyway. (Skivers, as they were known.)

Together, that made quite a lot of people who could, at that very moment, be spending money in Panface's shop. Which was why it was all the more concerning to Lee that Panface was visiting the school. Shutting up shop was costing Panface money, so he had to have left it for something important.

Lee couldn't help himself. 'What do you want the headmistress for?' he asked, suspecting he already knew the answer.

'My sales of sweets and crisps have dropped to next to nothing over the last few weeks. My shop used to be full of kids after school – so full that I had to limit the number allowed in at any one time, as you know yourself. But recently it's been completely empty. It's costing me a fortune. I've come to sort it out once and for all.'

'Maybe it's the new health drive. We can eat as much fruit as we want at lunchtimes now. Maybe that's it.'

'No. It's more than that. Kids don't suddenly stop eating crisps and chocolate just because they can get fruit at school. I have a pretty good idea as to what's going on and I'm going to see the headmistress about it.'

'Aw,' Lee said, although what he really meant was 'Oh no!' If the headmistress found out he would be in SERIOUSLY BIG trouble. He might even be suspended. Lee didn't want to imagine the reaction of his parents if that happened. This was serious.

'Anyway, I'm going to see her,' Panface said grumpily, and walked off.

For several seconds Lee's legs refused to move him from the spot where he was standing. His brain didn't have the spare capacity to direct them. It was too busy worrying.

How long would it take to reach the airport? Did he have enough money to buy a ticket to somewhere far away?

Somewhere like Rio de Janeiro, in Brazil. Wasn't that where criminals always headed when they needed to make a quick get-away? (Not that he was a criminal, of course, just a man on the run.) How much would it cost to get there? And would the weather be better than at home? Would his parents miss him? Would Rebecca? Would Will?

'Lee!'

He spun round, imagining that he was being called into the headmistress's office already.

But it was Will. 'What's spooked you?' he asked. 'You look like you've seen a ghost.'

'I think I might have. My own ghost. Because I'm dead meat.'

Will was alarmed. 'Why, what's happened?'

'It's Panface.' Lee related the conversation he'd just had with the angry shopkeeper. Will listened intently.

When Lee finished Will said, 'You've got to act quickly. No, on second thoughts, *we*'ve got to act quickly.

'You've got an idea?'

'Do you have any stock left?'

'Not really.'

'None?'

'Well I've kept a box or two of the marble stuff for

myself, in case I get hungry sometime ...'

'Never mind getting hungry. Here's what we need to do ....'

Chapter Twenty-Six

❟ Now then.' It was the next morning and The Ogre was wearing her most serious look. The sort that turned pants to putty, or something equally soft and squidgy but a lot more smelly. 'We've had a complaint.'

Lee hoped one of the parents had complained to the headmistress about The Ogre's breath. If so, it was not before time. Pupils nearly melted when she breathed on them. She was putting dragons out of business.

The old crone spelled out the nature of the complaint. 'Mr Travis, the gentleman who runs the shop most of you pass on your way home from school, and who I believe you call a much less flattering name, has experienced a significant downturn in business of late. It seems that, almost overnight, you've all stopped going to his store.'

She paused for effect and waited for a reaction. When none came she carried on.

'Now, judging from the wrappers in the bins out in the playground, it seems that you haven't stopped eating the sort of sugary and fatty rubbish you've always devoured so enthusiastically. So what I want to know is: where are you getting it from if you're not getting it from Mr Travis's shop?'

Everyone kept their eyes down.

'Well? Do I have any volunteers willing to explain what's been going on?'

No hands went up.

The Ogre strode up to Idle Ian's desk. If anyone was going to know where to get illicit grub it was him.

'Ian.'

'Yes?'

Idle Ian was sitting near the back of the class, so everyone turned around to focus their attention on him.

'I think it's fair to say that you normally provide a good proportion of Mr Travis's weekly income. When were you last in his shop?'

'Eh, about a month ago.'

'A month ago, eh? So what's the story, Ian? Where have you been going instead?'

The whole class was silent, awaiting Ian's next words.

'Where have I been going instead?' Idle Ian repeated.

'That's what I asked. Come on, answer me.'

Idle Ian blushed. He didn't like being the focus of attention. He preferred to be left alone. Ideally with a vast quantity of food.

The Ogre stood right in front of him and folded her arms.

'I'm still waiting, Ian.'

'I haven't been going anywhere,' Ian said.

The Ogre cackled cruelly. 'You haven't been going anywhere? Are you honestly telling me that you've given up eating sweets and crisps? Because I find that very hard to believe.'

She had a point.

'I have,' he told her. 'I've given them up for Ramadan.'

The Ogre raised her eyebrows so high that they almost became tangled in the ceiling lights. 'Oh really. For Ramadan?'

'Yes, eh, do you remember how in Religious Education you said that Ramadan is an important festival for Muslims? Well I thought I'd join in with it, what with this being the ninth month of their calendar.'

'But Ian, you're not a Muslim.'

'No ... that's true ... however, that's because I've never had the chance to be one.'

'What do you mean that you've "never had the chance"?'

Idle Ian didn't look too certain about where he might be going with this line of argument. 'I, eh ... well, the same as I've never had the chance to be a Hindu or an atheist or a Buddhist. I think it's important to explore other beliefs so that I'm able to make up my own mind which ones to follow.'

This was an impressive display from Idle Ian and an excellent (and much needed) recovery after a distinctly shaky start. His fellow pupils were witnessing a side to him that they had no idea existed. This was Idle Ian the wise philosopher.

The Ogre didn't know what to say. She'd never heard Ian utter so many words in a row before. 'That's a very interesting point, Ian. But I don't see what it has to do with where you get your chocolate supplies from.'

'That's easy. I haven't been getting any supplies. I've not been eating chocolate this last month since the first crescent of the moon became visible, which is the start of a month in the Muslim calendar, although it's a strange system because if it's cloudy you might have to wait a day or two before the month can start properly. And also, I don't know why they have Ramadan in September. They should do it in December because there's less daylight then, which would mean they wouldn't have to go for so long without food. Anyway, despite that, I've been fasting as a way of exploring the Muslim faith.'

'Really? You've been fasting? But I've seen you at school dinners.'

'Yes, that's right ... because I'm not fasting completely,

I've only given up food that's bad for me. Dieting you might call it. So I can still eat school dinners because they're very healthy.'

A few in the class looked at each other, wondering if The Ogre could possibly fall for this.

'Has it made much difference to you?' The Ogre asked, eyeing him up doubtfully.

'No.'

'You haven't lost any weight?'

'No.'

'And has it made you want to become a Muslim?'

'Eh, no.'

'I see. Well I suppose it's a good thing that you've made a point of exploring other religions.'

'Thank you. I think it's important to be agricultural.'

'Don't you mean multicultural? Unless you're thinking of becoming a farmer ...?'

'Oh. Eh ... yes. Multicultural.'

Having got nowhere, The Ogre gave up on Idle Ian and looked around for another victim.

'Lee.'

'Who, me?' Lee asked.

'There isn't anyone else in the class with your name, is there?'

Lee looked around, just in case someone had sneaked in without him noticing them.

'No,' he concluded.

'Then it must be you, mustn't it?' She stood before him, an intimidating sight. Lee could see right up her nose. Big hairs hung down inside, like abseiling ropes for bogeys. 'So where have you been buying your confectionery these last few weeks?'

'I haven't been buying any either. My mum's been on a diet because she ate loads on holiday and put on weight, and my family is supporting her by not eating the sorts of foods she's trying to cut out. But she's stopping tomorrow because she's done really well. Dad says she's got the figure of a model now and keeps pinching Mum's bum and ...'

'Yes, yes, Lee, I think we've heard enough of that.'

The Ogre moved on from Lee, who breathed a big, but silent, sigh of relief.

And so it went on for twenty minutes. But still The Ogre got nowhere. She wasn't able to extract a single piece of useful information. Lee only hoped that things were going as well in Will's class.

However, like a freshly cracked egg, The Ogre wasn't beaten yet.

'Well, if no-one is going to volunteer what's going on, I'll just have to search all your bags. Right, everyone, open your bags and place them on your desks.'

The kids in Lee's class did as they were instructed. Pencil cases and shoe bags crashed out into piles, along with two-week-old apple cores and tangerines that had grown blue with mould, rubbers pupils thought they'd lost, out-of-date notes to parents and even some money.

The Ogre patrolled the room, peering into each and every bag, even turning a few upside down again to make sure they'd been emptied properly.

Lee was just thankful this wasn't happening the previous day, otherwise he'd have been placing on his desk two bags either full of stock from *Lee's Mobile Tuck Shop* or full of the cash from selling it earlier in the day. He would have been in big bother whichever he'd been found with.

However, Lee's bag wasn't entirely free of what detectives on TV called 'incriminating' evidence – the sort that gained you a one-way ticket to prison. As he tipped it up, out fell two chocolate bars he'd been holding back in case of emergencies. He grabbed them and dropped them into his lap. From his lap he slid them into his pockets. He was fairly certain The Ogre wouldn't think of looking there. Who would be stupid enough to keep chocolate in their pocket where it would melt?

The Ogre was at the back of the class, raking through a particularly disgusting pile from a schoolbag belonging to a scruffy boy called Ben. Lee decided to make the most of the opportunity. He nudged Yasmin and then passed one of the bars to her under the table. 'That's for helping me with my Maths,' he whispered. 'Thanks.'

Yasmin looked surprised, and then delighted. She was about to reply when The Ogre stormed back to the front of the room and delved into the contents of those sitting around Lee's group of desks.

Of course, she didn't find anything.

'I don't know what's going on,' she roared as she finished inspecting the last bag, 'but I know something is. And I'm going to find out what.'

'How did it go?' Will panted, slowing down as he joined Lee at the school gate. He'd run out to meet his friend as soon as the bell had gone. 'Did the plan work?'

'Brilliantly! What about with your class?'

'Only just. Dominic got a bit mixed up with Lent. He said he thought Lent was when people borrowed things from you, not when you gave things up. But I think he got away with it. And Emma did okay with the Ramadan answer.'

'So did Idle Ian. He was superb.' Lee was starting to relax. 'What about you? Did you get asked anything?'

'No. Did you?'

'Yes. I used the helping-Mum-with-her-diet answer.'

'And it worked okay?'

'Seemed to.'

Passing classmates winked at Lee and Will, who smiled back. 'Thanks,' they said to those who'd had to answer questions.

'A bar of chocolate for each person,' Lee mused, 'and two for anyone who had to answer a question. Still, I suppose it was worth it.'

'Just as well you didn't bring any grub with you today.'

'I know. Can you imagine if I had and they'd done the bag searches? I'd have been hung, drawn and quartered, and then all my bits would have been tied to the school gate.'

'Yuck.'

'Exactly.'

'Well the thing is, if you're serious about stopping ...'

'Which I am.'

'... then everyone will need to go back to Panface's again, and if they do that then he'll be happy and won't moan to the school. And then the teachers will just forget about it.'

'Hmm. Just so long as no-one opens their mouth when they do go back to Panface's shop.'

'He'll be too busy to be interested in asking awkward questions. All he cares about is having his customers back. And anyway, he can't close you down because you've already shut up shop.'

Will was right.

'You know,' Lee said, 'maybe you should be in business, too. You've certainly got the brain for it.'

'No thanks. Not yet, anyway. Maybe when I'm older.'

They started walking home, taking their time like they used to.

'I can't believe you knew all that stuff,' Lee said.

'What stuff?'

'About Ramadan and the Muslim calendar. That was some crash course you gave Idle Ian. You should have heard him regurgitating it all. I was stunned. And so was The Ogre. She didn't know what to say. How did you learn it all?'

'It was in a library book I read on World Religions. It was quite interesting. I didn't even know there was such a thing as a Muslim calendar until I picked up that book.'

'It doesn't sound very reliable.'

'It's not. Which is why they use it mainly for religious

purposes. They use the same calendar as us for everything else. Ours is called the Gregorian calendar.'

'It just shows how people remember things when they need to.'

'Or when you're bribing them with a bar of chocolate.'

'Oh yes. That, too.'

Chapter
Twenty-Seven

Lee packed his tuck shop bags one last time and took them to school. Only this time his stock wasn't for selling, it was to pay bribes.

And as he handed out the remaining chocolate bars to his classmates, he actively encouraged them to start shopping at Panface's again. 'He's a nice guy,' he told his fellow pupils. 'He provides a good local service. Think how far we'd all have to walk to the supermarket if he closed down.'

This clearly struck a chord, because over the next few days a steady flow of customers returned to Panface's shop. By the end of the week, Panface had been forced to reintroduce his *no more than eight school pupils in the shop at any one time* rule.

It was still a worrying time for Lee. Any one of his fellow pupils could be caught off guard by Panface and accidentally reveal the real reason for his business having been so poor. A seemingly innocent question could be met with an equally innocent answer, but one that could spell disaster.

'So have you been dieting?'

'Are you kidding? No, I've been getting my sweets from this kid, Lee, at school, the one who almost ruined your business.'

That was all it would take. Lee almost felt guilty about what his actions had done to Panface's business. Almost, but not quite. Instead, he decided he had done Panface a big favour in a way. Competition to Panface's business could come at any time. A new shop could open right next door and what would Panface do then? Would his business be able to cope or would it go down the pan...so to speak? So all Lee had really done was give Panface a short shock and force him to improve his shop so that it could compete.

After ten days Panface still hadn't stormed up to the school again and Lee began to relax. He settled into a routine of school, followed by walking Rogan, doing his homework and then spending time with Will or Asad or both. Every Saturday he washed Holly Arthanthou's car, which didn't take long, and every other Wednesday evening he spent an hour or so working on Upa Blin Dali's garden. Having done the hard work when he started, all it needed now was a bit of weeding and the rubbish picked up that blew in off the street. It looked good these days. Lee didn't consider himself a gardener, nor did he want others to consider him as such, but he could almost understand why adults enjoyed it. There was something satisfying about the order he'd brought to the plants. Indeed, he didn't think of it as gardening now, more as art. A garden was like an artist's canvas. How you laid it out and looked after it determined the picture. Only, unlike a painting, a garden was a living picture, one that changed with the seasons.

Chapter
Twenty-Eight

And then one day, soon after, Lee's dad came home with some news.

The whole family was sitting at the dinner table when he announced it.

'It looks like we're going to be taken over,' he said.

'By aliens and mutants?' Lee asked, alarmed.

'No, no. By another company.'

Lee's mum was also concerned, though not about aliens and mutants. 'What about your job?' she asked. 'Do you think you might be made redundant?'

'Hopefully not. The other company's Internal Audit Manager left recently, so I should be given that position. And of course I'll be responsible for a bigger company once the takeover happens.'

'Oh, that's good.'

'Could even mean more money,' Lee's dad beamed.

'So who's going to run the company once the takeover happens?' Lee queried. 'Will it still be Wayne Scales?'

'Nope. I've no doubt he'll be making a fortune from sell - ing, though, so I wouldn't worry too much about him.'

'Why's he selling it?'

'He needs the money.'

'Really?'

'No.'

'Aw.'

'No, he's decided to move on to something new.'

'Such as?'

'Such as retirement. For the moment at least. It's a competitive marketplace, with lots of companies trying to do the same thing. Size matters now, so there are lots of businesses looking to make acquisitions – to buy other companies. That means Mr Scales should get a good price for the company when he sells it. And, as he would tell you himself if he were here, business is as much about knowing when to sell, as it is about knowing when to buy.'

This all made Lee feel much better about having closed the mobile tuck shop. He and Wayne Scales had both recognised a good time to open a business and a good time to let one go. It was no surprise. They were, after all, both entrepreneurial geniuses, just on a different scale.

And Lee had news of his own to impart. About a merger of a different kind.

'Do you know Jani Tor, the caretaker up at the school? And do you know Panface who runs the shop?' Both parents nodded. 'Well they're getting married.'

'Really?' Lee's mum said. 'Married?'

'Yes,' Lee confirmed. 'I know, I couldn't believe it either. A shopkeeper and a top spy, it's a strange combination, isn't it?'

'Spy?' Lee's dad queried.

Whoops!

'Guy, I meant. Top guy. Even though she's a woman...if you know what I mean ...'

'Eh, well, sort of ...'

'What I really mean is it's hard to see what she sees in him, isn't it? I mean he's hardly much of a looker.'

'It takes all sorts, Son,' Lee's dad told him. 'Beauty is only skin deep. Fortunately some people can see beyond it.'

'That's right,' Lee's mum said. 'Which is just as well for your dad.'

Your Thoughts

If you have any thoughts about this book, or if you simply want to complain about the jokes in it, please contact Keith via his website:

www.keithcharters.co.uk

where you can also get details on more books in the Lee series.

It's not every day that a part of your body explodes, but Lee's appendix does exactly that, landing him in hospital.

Soon after his operation, Lee is shocked to discover that evil Consul Mutants are trying to take over the world. Worse still, the hospital he is stuck in contains the portal they are using to invade Earth.

Other kids might quake in their boots at this news, but not Lee. He's determined to save the planet and comes up with a cunning plan to stop the aliens.

This is the story of a fearless boy battling against intergalactic odds for the sake of mankind. Lee's only weapon is his intelligence ... which is a pity.

Lee and the Consul Mutants
Keith Charters
ISBN 978-1-905537-24-2
(paperback, RRP £6.99)

Nothing is ever straightforward when Lee is around ... not even a summer holiday in Spain.

It ought to be a case of lazing by the pool, but Lee is soon spying on dodgy men in shiny suits and sunglasses, battling with a family that seems determined to ruin everyone's holiday and haranguing horrendous holiday reps.

With so much going on, how will Lee ever get a tan?

Lee's Holiday Showdown
Keith Charters
ISBN 978-1-905537-26-6
(paperback, RRP £6.99)

Lee has won the chance to be The First Child In Space. It's amazing what you can win these days by filling in a form on the back of a cereal packet!

Under the command of Captain Slogg, and with Sports Bob at the controls, Lee blasts off for the Moon on the trip of a lifetime. However, he and his fellow astronauts are not the only ones with their eyes on the big lump of cheese in the sky.

When disaster strikes, Lee faces the most important challenge of his life. If he succeeds he will return to Earth a hero. If he fails, he may not return at all.

Lee on the Dark Side of the Moon
Keith Charters
ISBN 978-1-905537-13-6
(paperback, RRP £6.99)

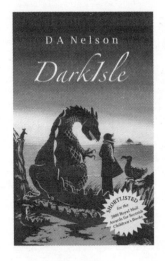

For 10-year-old Morag, there's nothing magical about the cellar of her cruel foster parents' home. But that's where she meets Aldiss, a talking rat, and his resourceful companion, Bertie the dodo. She jumps at the chance to run away and join them on their race against time to save their homeland from the evil warlock Devlish, who is intent on destroying it. But first, Bertie and Aldiss will need to stop bickering long enough to free the only guide who knows where to find Devlish: Shona, a dragon who's been turned to stone.

Together, these four friends begin their journey to a mysterious dark island beyond the horizon, where danger and glory await—along with clues to the disappearance of Morag's parents, whose destiny seems somehow linked to her own ...

DarkIsle
D A Nelson
ISBN 978-1-905537-04-4
(paperback, RRP £6.99)

The exciting sequel to the bestselling *DarkIsle*

Two months after she saved The Eye of Lornish, Morag is adjusting to life in the secret northern kingdom of Marnoch Mor. But dark dreams are troubling her and a spate of unexplained events prove that even with the protection of her friends—Shona the dragon, Bertie the dodo and Aldiss the rat—Morag is still not safe from harm ...

DarkIsle: Resurrection
D A Nelson
ISBN 978-1-905537-18-1
(paperback, RRP £6.99)

Twelve-year-old Bree McCready has a mission: she has just one night to save the world!

It starts when a clue inscribed on a Half-Heart Locket leads Bree and her best friends Sandy and Honey to an ancient magical book. With it they can freeze time, fly and shrink to the size of ants.

But they soon discover the book has a long history of destruction and death. And it's being sought by the monstrous Thalofedril, who will stop at nothing to get it.

Using its incredible powers, he could turn the world into a wasteland.

Bree, Sandy and Honey go on the run—hurtling off city rooftops, down neck-breaking ravines, and through night-black underground tunnels—to keep the book out of his lethal hands. Little do they know that the greatest danger of all lies ahead, in the heart of his deadly lair ...

Can Bree find the courage to face this terrifying evil, and to confront the secrets of her tragic past?

Bree McCready and the Half-Heart Locket
Hazel Allan
ISBN 978-1-905537-11-2
(paperback, RRP £6.99)

Everyone who came to the strange gym class was looking for something else. What they found was the mysterious Mrs Powell and Pashki, a lost art from an age when cats were worshipped as gods.

Ben and Tiffany wonder: who is their eccentric old teacher? What does she really want with them? And why are they suddenly able to see in the dark?

Meanwhile, in London's gloomy streets, human vermin are stirring. Ben and Tiffany may soon be glad of their new gifts. But against men whose cunning is matched only by their unspeakable cruelty, will even nine lives be enough?

The Cat Kin
Nick Green
ISBN 978-1-905537-16-7
(paperback, RRP £6.99)